Chapter 1. A Grave Problem

The Terrorist War in the Persian Gulf had escalated beyond all proportions.

Thankfully the major powers had deliberately played it very low key, only protecting each other's shipping, both East and West, within the Gulf itself.

The war zone had extended as far as the Strait of Hormuz with only minor incidents occurring outside.

This allowed the oil tanker fleets to remain outside the conflict area in relative safety under the umbrella of air superiority by the United Nations air force.

The pipeline from Kuwait to As Sohar on the Gulf of Oman coast was a financial failure due to continuous sabotage by Redexx terrorists. It was costing the oil companies billions of petrodollars just to get the crude oil to the heavy industrialised nations.

The major percentage of this cost was due to the heavy shipping losses in the Gulf waters.

Every ship that entered the Terrorist War zone was on its own. No insurance company had offered any risk cover since the United Nations had declared the waters west of the Strait of Hormuz "Aqua Non-Grata".

The Gulf was being left to religious fanaticism to carry out a self-elimination programme of genocide, or until all countries had enough of the killing.

Nobody had been able to stop this terrorism, so a commercial compromise had been reached several years ago.

The essence was that the terrorists could get on with it until they blew themselves to kingdom come with their suicide bombers, within their own boundaries and the Persian Gulf Terrorist War Zone.

But every time they put a foot outside those areas they were hit hard by the United Nations forces stationed around them.

Russian forces hit from the Caspian and Afghanistan areas.

Saudi Arabia and Syria from south and west of the zone.

India, Pakistan and Muscat from the south and east.

If the Terrorist War did anything positive, it united previous belligerents and put aside the old divides.

The Concordat was working satisfactorily, but at great cost to the oil industries and oil consuming nations.

There was of course a financial and commercial spin off as far as the British and American governments were concerned.

The major banks and insurance companies' embargo on insurance cover of vessels within the Persian Gulf had placed a responsibility an each country to protect their own registered shipping, which they gladly did, because the shipping companies paid a very high registration premium to their respective governments for this protection.

It is quite obvious to state that the premiums paid considerably offset any military costs involved and contributed enormously to each nation's defence budget.

When you also considered that the price of North Sea oil over the previous years had increased to the extent that this export alone had wiped out the preceding five years United Kingdom's balance of payments deficits, then Her Majesty's Government wasn't doing too badly out of the Terrorist War; these, of course, were only the published accounts.

All the warring nations relied to a considerable extent on the supply of modern armaments from the major powers. The Security Council embargo on the supply of armaments and spares into the declared war zone ensured that nothing at all could be supplied by any other nation. At least, that was the theory!

The war, the Concordat, the protection, in fact, the whole shooting match was costing money; but not to the major western nations.

In fact, all other countries not involved in the area were reaping the benefits. It was a classic situation where only the fighting nations were suffering. Enough oil was allowed to get out in fairly equal proportions from each Gulf State onto the world markets at a price, which maintained each country's war machine throughout each of the western nations' financial budgeting years.

The warmongers smiled broadly every morning at their breakfast tables when they read the newspaper headlines and listened to the latest information on the television and radio.

In the City they could quietly press a few keys on their computers and divert the odd fund here and there during the day then lodge it overnight with other colleagues in New York, Tokyo and Hong Kong.

For them, the Terrorist War was the best thing since sliced bread was invented.

This was the situation, when the Mini Cabinet of Her Majesty's Government met at Number Ten Downing Street for a general synopsis of the situation.

A serious development had taken place, which was going to cause a terrible imbalance in the whole situation. A policy decision at the highest executive level needed to be taken.

Within two minutes the Prime Minister adjourned the meeting until 1pm, at which time the Defence Secretary had been told to return and present his solution to the grave problem which was developing.

The Prime Minister reviewed the overall situation alone and decided that her afternoon meeting with the Defence Secretary would be held in secret. That way, the minimum number of people would know what they had decided.

She didn't want too many people in attendance. Perhaps just the two of them. If it didn't work out to her advantage she could always deny it afterwards.

Yes, that's what she would do.

Just the two of them.

That would suit her nicely.

She nodded to herself. Yes, very nicely indeed.

Chapter 2. Cold To The Core

The meeting was, as previously decided, in secret session with only two people present. No minutes were taken and no record of it existed afterwards.

"There is no doubt about it Prime Minister; there has been a sudden increase in Redexx Terrorist oil exports of refined oil into the World Market, through the Strait of Hormuz from their headquarters refinery at Bandar Abbas. The chemical analysis proves it beyond any shadow of doubt. This will extend the Terrorist War into the Indian Ocean States as far south as The Maldives.

"Are you sure about this?"

"Madam, there is no doubt about it, but we unfortunately cannot publicise otherwise we will definitely end up with egg on our faces.

Everybody else will deny it and we will have to agree that the intelligence was insufficient at the time, even though we know it to be corroborated and accurate.

Everybody else has already ensured that they know nothing about it as this will undoubtedly increase their military exports, including our own."

"So, what are you going to do about it?"

He held his dignified pose.

"There are two options available, Prime Minister. To stop the exports with our own independent strike at the heart of the problem and hopefully return to the status quo or, unfortunately, compromise our activities in the area by releasing the information to the United Nations for their action."

"Right, we will act independently, as we used to before joining NATO. Tell me how you are going to do it."

The Defence Secretary removed a red folder from his briefcase.

"We are going to clear the minefield laid by Redexx between Bandar Abbas and Ra's Ab Kuh in the Strait of Hormuz, in order to allow everybody's crude oil tankers out of the Gulf in sufficient numbers to match the Redexx oil production.

Within three weeks this will return to Gulf status quo. When that is achieved we will mine the area again.

We will allow three tankers to be lost, and then regretfully announce that escort duties can only be done with a large increase in registration premiums.

We expect status quo within two weeks after re-mining."

The Prime Minister looked at the Defence Secretary.

"I will not allow any of our forces to enter the Gulf for any mine clearing operation, so you can forget that idea."

He returned her gaze.

"Prime Minister, none of the British presence at the scene or any British military force will be used so we will not be implicated in any way.

Nothing will be traced back to us and should anyone even suggest that we did anything, we can prove that Her Majesty's Government had nothing to do with it."

"I sincerely hope so for your sake. I want the full details before I agree to any operation."

The Defence Secretary continued.

"When we disbanded CENTO in the early sixties, there were a number of obsolete atomic bombs stockpiled near Teheran airfield.

They were produced by Britain for the Shah of Persia at that time.

Most of these were returned to Britain in August 1965 and dismantled in the presence of the Geneva Verifying Committee.

I have a copy of the documentation for each weapon to prove this, the originals being held at The United Nations.

However, the Shah agreed to retain five of the bombs for contingency purposes should the occasion ever arise. When he was deposed these weapons were the subject of major concern and we mounted an operation to get them out in case anyone was tempted to use them.

Under the cover of the American attempt to release their hostages from the Teheran embassy, we sent in three SAS teams overland from Bushebr on the Southern Iranian coast, penetrated the airfield and took out the atomic cores from each weapon rendering them all useless.

The cores are now stored on the island of Gan in the Maldives. I intend to use these cores to blow a path in the minefield."

The Prime Minister looked at The Defence Secretary.

"Can they be traced backed to Britain by sampling any of the fallout debris?"

"No Prime Minister.

Not after we have doctored them.

They will have an atomic analysis commensurate with a dirty bomb constructed by another terrorist group."

"You had better be right about that. Your delivery method?"

"By aircraft. It will be flown to the island of Gan in the Maldives Archipelago in The Indian Ocean within three weeks.

The cores will be inserted into similar weapons then a low level raid will be flown along the desired path up to the deep-water channel at Bandar Abbas. The combined resultant explosion will cause sympathetic detonations of most of the mines in the minefield, and we estimate 96% of the existing mines will be cleared.

The remaining few will help us to control the Redexx tankers as they travel through the Strait."

The Prime Minister reviewed the idea privately for a moment.

"And public opinion, have you considered that?"

"Our first thought, Prime Minister.

We expect categorical denunciation at The United Nations Headquarters in the use of atomic weapons to clear the minefield.

Our delegate will table a motion calling for a ban on the future use of atomic devices. The Americans will back us up on this.

There will be a hue and cry for a few weeks then it will all die down."

There was a pause.

"Apart from the fine detail, the operation appears quite satisfactory but you will not use any of our aircraft or personnel. What is your intention?"

Again the Defence Secretary referred to his red folder.

"In simple terms, Prime Minister, we will have one of our old Vulcan aircraft stolen, presumably by an independent terrorist group, but it will be seen to be shot down immediately after takeoff by our defence systems.

We will be embarrassed by this incident, as it will indicate a weakness in our defences; but the evidence of its destruction will be obvious for everyone to see, including members of a Public Board of Enquiry, which I will instigate afterwards.

However, the aircraft will be flown to Gan directly after takeoff, and kept there until its mine clearing operation."

"Very well, Can you arrange a suitable cover for the crew as well?"

"Naturally, Prime Minister, it is already in hand."

There was a long silence in The Cabinet Room.

The Prime Minister spoke.

"One final point. I must emphatically insist that no trace at all can reflect on us whatsoever."

The last point was accompanied by a long cold glare.

"Is that perfectly understood, Defence Secretary?"

"Absolutely Prime Minister...

It has been arranged that after the last bomb drops from the aircraft it will explode on immediate impact with the surface of the sea, at exactly the same time as the other four explosions.

There will be absolutely no possibility of any evidence remaining to indicate the implication of Her Majesty's Government in this affair.

You have my categorical assurance on that."

She thought for a moment then gazed long and hard at the Defence Secretary.

She looked into his eyes, nodded once, and then looked down again at her watch.

"I have an appointment in ten minutes. We did not have this conversation. You must be very busy in your Affairs of State. Good day"

The Defence Secretary returned to his office, picked up the phone, pressed a green button and said only two words.

"It's on."

He then replaced the telephone receiver slowly back onto its cradle.

"By God, she's a cold hard woman", he remarked to himself.

"A very cold hearted woman."

Chapter 3. The Captain's Table

It wasn't Peter Barten's day. In fact it wasn't even his week.

He hated Mondays especially every other Monday.

Tomorrow was his signing on day at the unemployment benefit office to indicate that he was fit, dead keen and available for work. What a farce. Nobody would touch him, not even with a barge pole.

He wasn't just one of the great unemployed, but one of the great unemployable. During the last month he had landed a job a week but on each one had been given the big "E" after only two days.

The last one he held for a whole two hours before Ms Armstrong handed him his P45. He had only told her what to do with her job, and for some reason she'd taken umbrage, and in a very highhanded manner suggested he leave immediately.

Hence the escorted departure from the premises onto the pavement, by two extremely bulky security gentlemen.

He looked up at Lincoln Cathedral, now swathed in amber light from the big sodium floodlights sunk into the grounds all around the building. You could see it for miles.

He and his co pilot used to have a small competition when returning from Canada to see who could see the amber lights first from forty thousand feet.

The loser paid for the crew drinks.

But that was centuries ago.

He was now well and truly on the deck.

The great come down from head in the clouds to dragging in the gutter.

He was cold, wet, miserable and absolutely fed up with life. He wandered down the Lindum Hill hands in pockets, shoulders hunched, his tatty shoes scuffing along the pavement and stopped outside the Magistrates Court.

It was nearly two years ago when it all happened, but it was still as clear as a bell.

Remanded in custody until the Quarterly Assizes. The Judges procession to the Castle Crown Court after the Cathedral service.

"Ladies and gentlemen of the jury, have you reached your verdict?"

Guilty.

Lincoln jail.

Clunk.

The dull sickening thump from the cell door as it hit the steel framework then two miserable years of basket weaving and sewing mailbags.

"It's good preparation for meaningful employment, Barten" said the Prison Governor.

What employment?

He was better off inside at this rate. He kicked at an empty tin can in frustration and slouched down the hill into his favourite pub, The Old J B.

At least he could sit in the dry beside the fire opposite big 'Hiawatha', the pub totem pole carved out of six feet of solid pine trunk, listening to the resurrected jukebox as it churned out the oldies.

They must have known he was coming. At the moment it was belting out another recording of 'Fly me to the moon'.

If only.

He caught the barman's eye.

"Give us a half of the usual, Taff".

He was OK was Daffyd. A bit of a 'flower power', but a good soul.

He'd cheer you up when you were low in spirits and give a bit of tick on hard days, but nobody ever took advantage. The regulars would soon put paid to that!

He took his usual seat in the cubbyhole under the picture above the fireplace and looked around. The usual four young lads surrounded by their admiring ladies were chatting away about their latest cars and the hard work they all had to do.

He was pig sick of it.

He had four pence left and there they were flashing the fivers around and throwing beer down their throats as if their stomachs were on fire. He sipped his warm shandy to make it last and munched his soggy crisps which had fallen into the beer slops on the table.

He sighed heavily.

Monday night, no cash, no job, no birds, no prospects and down to his last half pint.

At least the gents were free.

"Some one's got it in for me all right," he said to himself, looking at the flames of the fire in despair.

"Care for a refuel Mr Barten?"

It was 'that' voice again. He looked up and saw a trimmed moustache surrounded by a supercilious face and well cut suit.

"I'm sure you could do with one. Real ale is much better than that rubbish you've bought for yourself.

Can't you afford a decent drink these days old boy?" said the moustache, as it placed a foaming pint on the wet beer mat.

He looked at it.

That beer, free though it was, represented bad news.

The last time he saw the moustache, and heard that voice, was about two years ago, at the Crown Court trial, but it wasn't giving away freebees then.

"I'll drink your rotten beer, then you can sod off and leave me alone."

"Now, now, old boy don't get nasty, I come on an errand of mercy."

It was that "old boy" bit that got me. Every time a winner in the cringe stakes.

"I hear you're a bit down on your luck." The moustache continued.

"What of it. When did you start giving out Sally Anne goodies?

You wouldn't help your best mate if you had one, so don't come that with me. Stick your pint."

I would have got up and left if it wasn't for his wallet, which he took out, removed fifty pounds and placed them in front of me. He obviously meant what he said.

"What's the catch?" I asked.

"None at all, I come to offer you a job. Help yourself to beer and a bit of the green stuff."

It didn't sound right, and I had to watch him. From past experience I knew this was a set up.

It was so obvious. You could read him like a book, and I'd have to be careful.

Still, no harm in listening, but he can stick his pint and his money. I wasn't so hard up that I'd take benefits from a 'snowdrop'.

Military police do not give out free beer and money, especially those who had stitched you up for a couple of years.

"Ok, I'll listen then decide."

He just looked at me, and that stupid grin started again.

"Oh dear, oh dear! I do think you've got it all wrong again Mr Barten.

We decide, and you listen; and in case you think otherwise just glance at this."

He held out a newspaper. It was locally printed and dated with tomorrow's date.

"It will be in the nationals the day after tomorrow, unless I stop it." was his casual remark.

I didn't believe it... the front-page story.

The main headlines splashed right across the page. With my photograph underneath, being held by two uniformed policemen.

The large print was bad enough, but the small print referred to my computer, downloaded with undesirable website material, now held in police custody as evidence.

"What the devil do you think you're doing?

This is all lies and you know it.

I haven't got a computer. I can't even afford a floppy disc!"

"You have now," he said.

"We supplied it for you. It came from another prosecution, and the owner got ten years.

Enjoy your stay in Lincoln Jail again, old boy."

He pulled out a folder from his bag, opened it up, and laid it on the table. Then he put on a large stupid pair of spectacles that made his face look like a cow with wind.

"Let's have a little look at your brilliant career as a brylcreem boy, shall we."

He read from the folder:

"Flight Lieutenant Peter Archibald Barten, Royal Air Force. Splendid service for seven years as a jet pilot, finishing up on fourjets.

Big car, big bird, big overdraft, big drinks, big headed and pig headed.

Apprehended by the Lincolnshire Police after a drink/drive accident July 2005.

Held in custody overnight August 2005, same charge.

Knocked down and seriously injured a young girl on a pedestrian crossing in Lincoln High Street, January 2006 and finally cashiered from the service, dishonourably discharged on 23rd February 2007.

Now, here you are, old boy, you've just lost four little jobs in as many weeks, and tomorrow you could be charged for downloading internet nasties because of your perverted mind.

You won't last ten days in jail let alone ten years when we tell everybody else what you did with the files."

I was half way across the table, going for his throat, when the other two just appeared and sat down either side of me. They were like two streaks of greased lightning.

They casually placed their elbows on the table, and gripped my wrists in mid flight, then, with a sickly grin on each of their faces, bent their arms slowly forward and pinned me to the top of the table.

I was locked solid and couldn't move a muscle. Their hands were the size of dinner plates, and their shoulders looked as if they had come straight out of the body building adverts you see in the magazines to convert wimps to a big meaty 'Beach Adonis'.

"You always were a bit hasty weren't you Barten? You'll never learn.

My two colleagues did their apprenticeship on the shore patrol along the dockside in Portsmouth. They didn't bother with pickaxe handles or knuckle-dusters and always worked as a pair.

They found that working in the usual patrol of four interfered with their powers of human destruction."

I was beginning to get the message. My arms were turning a nice shade of blue. It was time for initiative.

"Taff, be a good chap will you, and give my newfound friends a beer each."

He looked across and saw me with my new 'friends'.

"My pleasure.

Brown ale for the lovely big boys.

Coming right up now."

He put two pint glasses and a quart bottle on a tray and meandered over to our table.

He stood limpish beside the one on my right.

"Now then, who shall I serve first?"

He then gave him one of his special smiles, scratched his earlobe with the fingers of his left hand, and at the same time smashed the thick solid quart glass bottle as hard as he could on the back of the hulk's head.

The beer bottle exploded in a spray of brown ale and broken glass.

I thought at the time, what a waste of good beer, but it had the desired effect.

There was a glazed look in his eyes for a couple of seconds during which he relaxed the grip on my right arm.

I pulled as hard as I could, wrenched it free, then smashed my fist repeatedly into the other hulk's face, as hard and as fast as I could, until it was a mass of blood and bones...

My fist that is!

Hulk Two, grinning at me, leant over and took out the handkerchief from the top pocket of my jacket and wiped the blood from his face.

... It was my blood, from my agonising fist, or what was left of it!

He just sat there and grinned, showing off his big white teeth like a toothpaste advert, whilst my poor hand throbbed in agony.

Hulk One shook his head, recovered himself and slowly looked round.

The grin started as his big meaty hand stretched up and gently lifted Taff's tie from the front of his shirt.

"I eat little boys like you for breakfast," he said, as he stood up and raised him four inches from the bar room floor, then slowly swung him from side to side.

One of the regulars saw what was happening.

"Hey, fellas, look.

They've got our Taff."

The pub went very quiet.

"Oh no they haven't. Not while I'm here," came another cry.

A fully loaded pint glass filled with best brew was flung right across the room, and smashed into Hulk One's neck.

"That's for starters mate."

A second glass flew across the bar from the other corner and disintegrated two inches higher up on the crown of his head.

"And that's for seconds."

That started a regular fusillade of beer bottles, glasses, glass ashtrays, chairs, tabletops and the various objets d'art lying around the pub, which all smashed and shattered against Hulk One.

Soon he was soaked in a blend of real ale, draught beer and bottled beer. His hair and clothes a mass of broken glasses, shattered bottles and splintered wood.

There was silence in the pub for two seconds.

The moustache examined his fingernails carefully for any minor beer blemish or stain.

Hulk Two grinned at me with sadistic pleasure, as my body racked in agonies from my own pulverised fist, and Hulk One slowly let Taff down in order that he could breathe again.

He shook his hair with his left hand, took out a thick piece of glass ashtray, which was imbedded there and turned round to face the crowd, now hushed in expectation.

Hulk Two spoke. "D'ya wanna hand?"

"Nah, there's only ten of them.

Ten an' an nahf if you count Mr Flower Power."

He dipped the piece of glass into a bowl of tomato ketchup sauce lying on the bar, like a stick of celery into salt, popped it into his mouth, and with a satisfying smile crunched it with his teeth until it was powder, then swallowed it.

He had the decency to wipe the excess ketchup from his mouth afterwards with a convenient serviette lying on top of an adjacent table, and with a smile that would have made the Mona Lisa jealous, advanced slowly towards them all, with fingers and thumbs outstretched and flexing gently, ready for the gulping throats out in front of him.

"Hell's teeth, we're dead," said a voice.

"I'm off," said another.

"Me too," said a third.

"Sorry, Taff, you're on your own mate," was the general cry, as the mass exodus crushed through the door to the roadway outside.

The pub emptied in seconds.

It was as if someone had said the free beer was outside on the pavement.

Hulk One watched them vanish, stopped, looked at me, smiled, and then sat down beside me.

The moustache polished his fingernails on the lapel of his coat.

"Now, Mr Barten, a little present for you..."

And they were fast and heavy. It was classic.

The one on the left lifted me upright by the use of my hair and his right hand. His friend grabbed my beer glass and threw the contents into my face.

The next thing I saw was his bunched up fist two inches from my nose, travelling fast in my direction.

The last thing I felt was his arm around my neck, in a very professional choke hold, before I blacked out.

Taff can remember them dragging me out on my back by my worn out old shoes, to a car in the square near the front door, and chucking me into the boot like a sack of Lincolnshire potatoes.

They both returned, looked around the empty pub, now littered with rubbish and smelling of spilt beer. The jukebox was still working its guts out, trying to get Frankie into orbit, on his way to the moon in the key of C major.

They lifted the six feet high solid wood totem pole carving of Hiawatha, turned towards the juke box and threw the reluctant Indian across the length of the pub into the flashing amber lights induced by the cacophony of noise, and Frankie blew up as he reached the high note of his song.

He had flown his last trip to the moon.

"Never did like him," said Hulk Two, as he turned and walked towards the now trembling body of Taff.

"Night night, flower boy," he said, gently placing an artificial rose into his chattering teeth; then left him on his favourite tartan carpet surrounded by the litter of a one sided punch up in what was once the best-looking pub in Lincoln.

* * *

It only took me three days to recover.

Three days of agony and hell.

"Good morning, Mr Barten."

I can vaguely remember Cathedral bells ringing, a hotel room, a very pleasant looking young lady, a breakfast tray and the smell of a cooked breakfast and a pot of hot tea beside me.

"Welcome back again to the real world."

Yes, it was true... breakfast in bed... unbelievable, but true.

"Good morning Peter."

I looked up at the hazy figure in front of me and with great difficulty managed to focus an eye. It was a man in a Crombie overcoat.

"Thank you Jacques, see you tomorrow morning," he said to the moustache and his two twins, who were present obviously for my protection whilst in a state of exhausted unconsciousness.

"I think we'll both have a pleasant cup of tea together and a little chat," he said to me as he filled two china cups.

"Would you like a little job Peter, reflecting your previous skills, foolhardiness and expertise?" He stirred his teacup.

I groaned. It was back to the Job Centre again.

"I've already done all the gent's loos in Lincoln. Are we moving further afield then?" I asked.

"In a manner of speaking... Yes.

Tomorrow you will be told exactly what we are going to do with you over the next few weeks, but to put it briefly, it will require a bombing raid operating from an island in the Indian Ocean.

Our police friends tend to be a bit dramatic, but after the briefing tomorrow morning you will have as much information and assistance as you need. It's a big operation and very detailed.

Your task is to fly a new Display Vulcan from Waddington, to the remote island of Gan in the Maldives for the strike."

He added another spoonful of sugar into his tea carefully inspecting the surface as he slowly stirred it in with his teaspoon.

I woke up very quickly. "I don't believe this. You're joking"

He looked at me.

"Oh no, Peter, we're quite serious.

In fact not only are you going to fly it, but beforehand you have got to steal it from the dispersal, take off in the dark with no lights, be shot at from the ground with an anti aircraft gun, catch fire and then simulate a crash about ten miles from the base.

The papers will report the complete loss of the aircraft and all its crew, but by that time you'll be over the Sahara Desert, having breakfast and a long cool drink.

It's all in the folder:

I suggest you spend the next few hours reading it, then we'll get down to business."

I was left on my own for two hours before they took the folder away. If I'd heard about this three days ago I wouldn't have believed it, but now that I knew what was going on it would take more than three snowdrops to keep me out.

I was in this for keeps. It was a lot better than my old Royal Air Force job, and what made it more attractive, the beer was free!

Afterwards, 'Crombie Man' picked up his mobile and spoke quietly into it.

"Ma'am, I think we've found our man. He seems quite absorbed in the operation."

"Well done", said the voice.

"Commence tomorrow as planned, and report daily as agreed. Goodbye."

He locked across at the 'moustache'.

"Send your two thugs to bed. We won't need them. I'm sorry to disappoint them but we shall not require their sadistic pleasures this evening."

The moustache sighed wearingly.

"Such a shame. I had great plans for him in Colchester. We would have had the cleanest toilets in Britain.

I'll have my fine friend one day. There's plenty of time yet.

One little slip, and off he goes to the land of ten mile cross country runs, carrying telegraph poles on his miserable shoulders, before breakfast."

He was going to wait a long time though. He never did catch me.

Chapter 4. Delta Force

I met my number two the following day.

They had found him scratching out a living in Cornwall around the old Beevor tin mine. Ray Preston was his name and he had received the same initiation ceremony as I had.

My drinking partners used the same newspaper article, this time in the Penzance Gazette but they had changed the routine slightly, presumably to stop themselves getting too bored. It was the left fist to the nose this time.

"Peter, this is Ray. He's seen the folder and knows as much as you do so we won't waste any time. You will both stay in this complex until we are ready and when we see you again it will be at Gan.

Your timing schedule is here, and please stick to it. Every location is marked on the plan. Be there as requested as most of your visitors have to travel in from outside sources.

If you have any problems please call us on the portable televiewer. I suggest you get acquainted."

After that he was gone. No doubt to the control room behind the mirror.

"What's your background, Ray?"

"Eight years in the Air Force, ending up on tankers for a while. Then a ground job training young kids and turning them into airmen. I left just after that."

I looked at him.

"And the rest. Where does the evil little moustache come into your lifestyle? I presume you're not exactly here for the glamour and bon-a-vie that comes with the job?"

The groan, the usual sigh, the long pause.

"It was referred to as grievous bodily harm. I call it severe provocation by an objectionable little darling.

He was the lucky one.

He only visited hospital for half an hour, and they gave him a 'heroic' bandage and a Teddy Bear.

I ended up with Monsieur Jacques le Boustarde for the rest of my natural. He's like a huge festering boil that turns up every year right in the middle of one's derriere, as they say in the car adverts."

"Where did they find you?" I asked.

He continued.

"I was working in the Beevor tin mine in Cornwall, trying to escape from the world, and was just having my lunch when this big gorilla came up and flattened my sandwiches into the dirt with his boot.

I couldn't get up to thump him one because the other thick ape held my head down with one hand and crumpled my coffee flask with the other. They were gently lifting me up with their finger tips when the rest of the shift came to help me.

There were thirty of them.

Big hard blokes wearing hob nailed safety boots with steel toe caps, all holding pick axes, shovels, pit props and leather belts with solid brass buckles.

It was a massacre.

It lasted less than a minute.

There was blood all over the place.

It took a fleet of ambulances to carry them all to Penzance hospital. I can vaguely remember seeing two sets of grinning white teeth through the swirling dust, just before they threw me up the lift shaft."

"Surely, you mean down?" I queried.

"No, pal. Up!

Going upwards with the stop at the top was all right, but coming downwards with the sudden stop at the bottom caused me concern.

I was about to end up like Mrs Trevellick's best strawberry jam spread all over the concrete floor, when le Boustarde casually suggested that it might be in their best interests to catch me, as it would mean searching for somebody else if they didn't.

They relented. I got flung against the wall of the mineshaft and then dragged on my back up to the surface by the steps.

All nine hundred and fifty of them...

And they were best salmon sandwiches as well!

I'd made them myself.

How did they get you?" he asked, rubbing the back of his head.

I told him the whole story.

And that's how I met Ray. Both of us a pair of washed out dead beats, slung out the Royal Air Force by the scruff of our necks, and recruited from the pits of Civvy Street by a nasty little piece of work, with a French sounding name, that made Inspector Clouseau look intelligent.

"As a matter of interest", Ray said, "Why do you think they've selected us for this job, when there are others a darn sight more competent to carry it out?"

"Don't get too excited, and try not to think about it," I replied,

"... but on the great balance sheet of life there is such a thing called 'expendable and disposable assets', and I think we may come into that category."

There was the hasty filling of two glasses, and we drank to a common toast:

"An airman's farewell to the poison dwarf."

There was a series of discussions and mini conferences after that.

Our first visitor was a pin striped City gentleman complete with briefcase and bowler hat. He was good.

You see them on the television walking in droves to and from London, but what he didn't know about oil and money and the power and control that they can both give, you could write on the back of a postage stamp.

We knew of course all about the tankers and the prices and the activities in the Middle East area, but we didn't know about the secret deals across the satellite links, the influence that the big organisations have on the small countries, especially in the third world, the power and control in the hands of a few people and how it is possible for the crude black stuff to radically change our way of thinking... particularly in politics.

Add into that a religious element and you begin to think in terms greater than the price of petrol at the pumps.

By the time he had finished, both of us were convinced that the only way that the Terrorist War was going to end was by helping in the mine clearance activity in the Persian Gulf.

Before he departed he passed a piece of paper to us with the name of a company on it.

"If you can get a few thousand pounds on that by nine thirty tomorrow morning neither of you will have to work again for the rest of your lives," he said with a wink.

I groaned. It was like receiving a blank cheque with lots of noughts on it from a bookmaker and I could do nothing about it!

A rather formidable military type followed him. He advised us of the activities of the other Major Powers involved in the Gulf.

The United States were clearing the southern Iranian coastline. The French were tasked with clearing a path from Bahrain to Kuwait and our job was to clear the Strait and up as far as Bandar Abbas.

Specific buffer strips had been set up between these areas to reduce the fallout effect, which will clear within five weeks, after which time it would be safe to sweep with the mine hunters.

By using a mixture of nuclear shocks and normal sweeping he told us that the Gulf could be 96% clear of all mines within three months, and that the rest could be left to the mine hunters.

After the first week we were both very fit and finished with all the chat shows.

The bunker, we found out later, was fifty feet under the ground a few miles east of Lincoln and it was linked to the main regional bunker by a staff service tunnel, and that's where we both went for the second week of our training.

We swished along on a rail pathway in an underground rail coach on comfortable rubber tyres, just like the Paris Metro, and about half an hour later stopped just to the south of Lincoln.

We had heard about these Nuclear Bunkers, but this was the first time that we had seen one. It was built into the Lincoln Edge Escarpment, underneath the Cliff Villages that ran north to south along the Grantham Road.

It was an enormous area completely floodlit, a huge cavern with a circular roof like the inside of the Albert Hall.

It was as bright as the Blackpool illuminations but without the people. A vast complex of railway lines and carriages - and there in the middle, on two flat wagons, a Vulcan bomber.

"Good Lord, look at that." Raymond responded first.

It was unbelievable.

I just gazed at it.

I can still remember that vision to this day. It was bright silver from refuelling probe to fin top and glistened in the arc lights.

The main wheels were up. The fuselage was resting on the nose and a special set of tail wheels, each set into their own flat wagon, and the wings spread across the railway lines resting on wooden cradles.

It was like a low pass across an airfield - a very, very low pass!

The last time that I had seen a silver Vulcan was the BCDU aircraft at the RAF Finningley air display in the 1960's, but this was much more impressive.

"How did you get that down here?" I asked.

"Don't ask too many questions for the moment, just accept the fact that it is here. You will find out a lot more tomorrow," our man for the day told us.

"We must start getting you both ready for your flight. Now watch the aircraft carefully."

He turned to an electrical distribution box on the wall, and switched off half the lights.

The colour changed to a light grey.

"Keep watching."

He switched off more lights, and as he did so the aircraft gradually became lighter shades of grey ,eventually to the point where it was very difficult to see.

Ray spoke first.

"I assume if this occurs with angstrom units, it will also occur with other points in the spectrum, including microwaves?"

"That's quite correct. I think you've got the point.

This aircraft is very difficult to see at night with the naked eye, and cannot be picked up by RADAR. Their transmissions are affected by the silver film, which has a high refractive index, the phase angles alter around the aircraft surface, and nothing gets reflected back to their receivers.

All microwaves, x-rays and the vision spectrum frequencies are totally refracted by the silver atoms, and pass out the other side the leeward side.

It would take a supersonic bat flying at ninety thousand feet to find this aeroplane.

Shall we proceed?"

I turned to Ray with a slight bow.

"After you, my good fellow!"

Ray, elegant as ever, bowed slightly lower.

"Oh no, my dear chap, after you."

I smiled and we both walked towards our new aircraft.

The only one of its kind in the world and one of the last two flying Vulcans.

Chapter 5. Modifications

If you were to take a short wheel base Landover of 1950 vintage, which has been used by a Welsh sheep farmer constantly for about thirty years, strip it down, change the chassis, the wheels, the bodywork, take out all the useless equipment, put in brand new modern gear and a souped up engine, theoretically you could end up with the latest Range Rover model.

Well, that's the equivalent to what we had:

The wings had new curved leading edges that smoothed their way into the fuselage.

The enlarged engines, both set into the wing roots had been developed from Concorde.

All the rivets had been replaced with flush rivets that now produced smooth top and bottom surfaces.

The bomb aimer's window no longer existed, which now resulted a smooth under surface to the fuselage.

The refuelling probe was still in position but that seemed to be the only attachment. Everything else had been removed, to give a very smooth gloss finish.

Inside the cockpit, the two pilots' seats had been taken out, and from what I could see, a lot of the old type of instruments were replaced with visual display units and glass fibre connections.

There was one pilot's seat centrally placed with a small electronic joystick close to each arm.

On the fuselage walls at each side of the seat, mounted on hinged racking, were the various switches for fuel pumps, cabin pressurisation systems and the other functionary systems with which to operate the aircraft.

On the front panel to the left of the main instrument VDU was a Decca satellite navigation VDU with an additional diskette programme facility, which could be used for pre-programmed auto pilot control.

The centre window panel had a head up display fed by the infra red television camera set in the front of the fuselage. Who needed daylight now with this lot to do the work?

The rest of the cabin had been altered likewise.

No longer the cramped quarters for a generation of rear crew to either sweat or freeze in.

Gone were the three rear facing seats and the old fashioned navigation equipment to be replaced with two comfortable folding chairs, that converted to a bunk facing two computer screens.

The space where the bomb aimer's window used to be was now a small galley.

All we needed now were curtains on the windows and a stewardess… but even the poison dwarf couldn't have got us those.

"So where did this machine come from?" I asked.

It was the chief controller who told us.

"The last flying Vulcan was sold to the Air Museum at Bruntingthorpe, and is now acting as a display aircraft. We can't use that for obvious reasons, and we weren't allowed to use the Waddington Vulcan, so we had a look around for another one in good condition.

It's for special operations, under the cover of being a second display aircraft.

We found it at the Air Museum at Winthorpe, just to the east of Newark, and brought it here to the bunker for a few modifications.

"How the devil did you get it here?" Ray asked.

"It was quite simple really. We removed the engines and all the unnecessary equipment that needed replacing.

It was then lifted up clear of the ground by hydraulic jacks.

We took off all the undercarriage bogies and wheels, then placed two canvas slings around the fuselage fore and aft of the delta wing, lifted it out with our big Sikorsky helicopter-crane, flew it here and lowered it down through the roof opening into the bunker.

We played a good trick on Bill."

"Who's Bill?" I asked.

"Oh, that's the chap at Winthorpe who looks after it.

He eats, sleeps and dreams Vulcans, especially 594.

We arranged all this with the Air Museum Staff, but they decided not to tell him.

After we cleared the site, we air-lifted in a one third scale model of the Vulcan as a replacement. It was the one they used for the film Thunderball.

When Bill arrived to do his Saturday duty they told him that it had shrunk in the rain the week before. Apparently he's still sitting there looking at it, muttering incoherently into his beard."

"Lucky feller," I said, "at least he is out of this madhouse."

"Don't worry, it can only get worse.

Have a look at the registration plate next time you go into the cabin, just above your head as you go up the door.

We keep it inside for security reasons but you can make out the old RAF number, XH 594, and the new UN registration VFORS.

It has at least another five years before the next major overhaul, so do your best, try not to bend it too much."

Working on the principle that I was going to be inside it at least for the foreseeable future, I tended to agree with his last sentiment.

The man for the day provided us with the various software disks, which we fed into appropriate equipment for exercise purposes. By linking these into the main computer control, and feeding a laser disc into the head up display unit we had a perfect simulator.

We could even start and operate the engines, but on reduced power. Neither of us fancied flashing across the bunker at over five hundred miles per hour.

We both lived, ate and slept in that aircraft for over a week. With of course the usual visits to our bunker and controllers for the daily chat. By the end of the second week we were both highly confident that we could fly it for real.

It would soon be put to the test.

We weren't to know it but ours were not the only activities that week. Even if we did have access to the outside world, I doubt if we would have noticed anything different.

* * *

Jack Marrily stormed into the Dog and Duck at Fulbeck, a village to the north of Grantham.

The pub was the centre of activity at this time of day. He just said three words and that was enough.

"NIREX are back."

You could have heard a pin drop. The villagers had just won a very successful campaign to get NIREX away from the old airfield, where they had been digging core samples for low level nuclear waste.

They had hoped it was for all time, but not according to Jack.

"They moved in last night, and now they're digging the trenches ready for the waste.

There's already a truck load of bags and barrels at the north end of the airfield ready for burying. There are warning signs all round the area.

I've just been told that I can't even plough my own fields."

The evening papers got the story immediately, plus some very early letters to the editor on how you couldn't trust a politician as far as you could throw one, and as soon as they got re- elected back into power they would do just what they wished, irrespective of what they promised in their manifestos.

It made no difference.

The chairman of the L.A.N.D. organisation organised the village protesters again, but all the steam had gone out of them now that the disposal had commenced.

The blockades to the airfield were non effective. NIREX just took another route in.

There was no back up from the other proposed sites like the last time NIREX did their exploratory drilling.

It was a case of NIMBY. They weren't particularly concerned as long as the stuff wasn't landed on them.

The motion tabled in the Commons by the local MP was shouted out.

"Hard luck Grantham and Sleaford.

Drew the short straw did you?

Shame, never mind. It'll be soon be Christmas...

Everybody will soon forget it..." etc, etc.

It would take a miracle now to move them to a deep offshore site, which was what everyone had hoped for.

Fulbeck was a very unhappy village.

* * *

Exercise Midland Plain was in full swing, all down the east coast of Lincolnshire and Humberside.

Forces representing an invasion and landing by beach and parachutes were preparing for their annual Territorial Army exercises.

Embarkation and emplaning would take place at various NATO depots in Holland and Germany over the weekend ready for the big move back to East Anglia on Wednesday evening and early Thursday morning.

The objective: to land and penetrate certain military establishments along the east coast. It was as real life as it could be made in the circumstances and tended to be hard work and enjoyable.

At Hereford, two SAS teams received their instructions for the weekend operation.

Move up and reconnoitre Sunday afternoon. Penetrate early Monday morning. Stay low for 24 hrs. Make the hit early Tuesday morning.

Target: the big AWACS base at Waddington, Lincolnshire.

They had not been done since the new squadrons moved in. It was time they received a shot up the backside.

No live rounds this time, blanks only. They quietly got on with the preparation and planning.

Squadron leader David Bershaw, Royal Auxiliary Air Force, briefed his men for the forthcoming exercise.

"We can expect enemy forces early Thursday morning backed up by ground attack aircraft. Our job is airfield defence.

Two units will revert to blank shells for exercise purposes, the other two will retain live and tracer rounds.

All guns will be loaded for the exercise, but only blanks fired on the night.

We will all take a part to make sure each person has experience of manual firing.

Any questions?"

There were a lot, and they were all answered, because this was the first time this year that the mobile, radar operated Oerlikon rapid firing airfield defence guns captured during the Falklands campaign would be used in a major exercise.

"We will commence our own station exercise on Sunday evening at 1800 hrs as planned and terminate with exercise Midland Plain."

Captain John I Majors of the United States Air Force, based at Barksdale had made all his preparations for the annual open day and air show.

He had sent off the visiting aircraft operations signal to the Vulcan display flight commander.

It gave details of airfield timings, frequencies to use, arrival and departure times and a list of display times for the aircraft on air display.

If it was anything like last year the crowd should top one and a half million.

When the signal was received by Waddington the aircraft would be prepared by the ground crew for the trans-atlantic trip on Thursday morning, to arrive two days later for the ground display landing.

The air display was usually very impressive and always popular with the crowds, even though the aircraft was older than most of them!

* * *

On Monday afternoon we were taken to the small interview room for our final briefing.

Pinned on the wall were a high definition photograph of an airfield, and a map of the immediate countryside.

We were told exactly what to do and what to expect.

No luggage, no personal effects, strip off and shower.

Put these on.

It was impersonal to say the least.

"There is a car outside that will take you to the drop off point.

The two men with you will get you through the fence and to the fuel pipeline two hundred yards from the aircraft then you're on your own.

Good luck."

And that was it.

After they had gone, Jacques le Boustarde entered the room.

"Well, can they do the job?"

The Controller locked at him.

"Oh yes, they can do it all right. There's no doubt about that.

Your problem is to do with security. Don't you trust them?"

The smile developed slowly.

"Not in the slightest. I'm pleased they're operating from Gan as far away from normal human beings as possible.

I wouldn't give that pair a wet firework, let alone five atomic bombs, and I still wouldn't feel safe in my bed at night."

Then he looked at the map on the wall.

"And another thing, they'll be damn lucky to get away with this caper tonight.

I'm not placing any bets on them getting away with that aircraft."

He screwed his cigarette end into the ashtray until it was just a mangled mess of dirty brown tobacco and ash; then took a long look at the black remains, the smoke still curling up, turned on his heel, said nothing and walked out of the room.

The Controller picked up the green telephone.

"They're on their way, Sir. Everything going as planned."

The reply was cordial.

"Well done, Andy. I suggest you get off to Gan now. Keep in touch via Skynet.

You've done a good job in the circumstances.

Well done".

Andrew Allan had been in the United Nations service for over five years, and was now the leading controller for their forces in the Gulf. He knew the risks involved with this operation, and had trained the two 'new boys' as best as he could in the time available.

He picked up his case and walked thoughtfully to the underground rail-link with Lincoln Central Station, and sat in the carriage with the other staff.

The doors closed, the train rumbled off, and Andy was on the first leg of his journey.

To Heathrow by train, London to Riyadh in their own UN Concorde, then onwards to Gan by Tristar.

The passenger sitting opposite him was reading the Lincolnshire Echo. He could see the headlines across the front page as it was being held up in front of him:

"Terrorists Attack the Dubai Palm. Hundreds killed."

He was used to it. Nothing had changed.

He wasn't going back to the war.

He'd never left it.

Chapter 6. A Very Hasty Departure

The evening watch at the control tower thankfully had been quiet after the day's activity. The Duty Controller had just seen the giant Boeing AWACS, call sign Awacs 14, airborne onto the northern patrol over the ice cap. It wouldn't be back until morning then the next watch could see it down.

Awacs 24 and Awacs 15 were returning this evening and Awacs 06 early in the morning. The display Vulcan in its new silver livery had returned from its refit and was being prepared for the Barksdale trip. It was fully fuelled up, including the additional external fuel tanks, and parked on its usual dispersal pan, across the airfield beside the Sleaford road.

The Royal Auxiliary Air Force controller in charge of the station defence guns had checked in on the ground radio frequency as part of the defence exercise.

The airfield was acting as a major diversion airfield for East Midlands International Airport and as such would remain open all through the watch. Wingco Ops had done his evening check on them so they could relax a bit and put the coffee on.

To the southern end of the airfield the two AWACS squadrons were preparing for the exercise later in the week. A short notice signal had been received earlier on during evening calling them both onto a six hour take off alert. It had been expected sometime during the week but unfortunately arrived a day earlier than the engineers had planned for.

The air traffic log was uneventful in that it recorded the normal air traffic messages from passing aircraft, civil landings and take offs and the usual practice emergency messages from student pilots at the Royal Air Force College to the south of the airfield.

The airfield was slowly transferring to nocturnal activity with the night duty staff maintaining routine procedures until the next day watch arrived.

"Message from Awacs 06, Sir. It's due in at 0100 hrs. I'll mark it up on the board."

"Thank you, corporal."

"Tower this is Gunsite 4 checking in."

"Roger, Gunsite 4, you're loud and clear."

The phone rang.

"I've got tomorrow's flying programme for you... It was all routine communications.

At midnight a car travelling towards the airfield stopped about a mile short of the airfield. Four people dressed in black coveralls, gloves, balaclava helmets and darkened faces emerged and disappeared into the blackness of the night.

By quarter past the hour we were under the barbed wire fence and had cut our way through the inner trip wire. The fuel pipelines from the refinery on the coast linking with the station main control valves was about two hundred yards ahead of us with the Vulcan beyond. Our two companions led the way crawling between the bomb shelters, across the grass, rolled across the road and then slid underneath the fuel pipes running to each of the dispersals. The one on the left carried on for fifty yards then turned a sharp right straight for the Vulcan.

I looked at my watch. Half past midnight.

We had to be inside the aircraft within fifteen minutes before the patrol arrived.

"Best of luck," said our two companions and they were gone.

The security lights were facing outwards flooding the surrounding area with bright amber light.

"I'll go first, Ray."

I grabbed hold of the pipe and pulled myself along on my back.

There was just enough clearance underneath to do it. We used as much of the shadow created by the lights as we could. Timing was essential as the next patrol was due about one o'clock.

It was hard work as neither of us had much experience of crawling backwards, upside down, in sweaty coveralls in the middle of the night through long, cold and wet grass. The only crawling I was used to was a pub crawl, not this stupid lark.

It took us ten minutes to reach the dispersal. At the end of the pipe there was about fifty yards of bare concrete to cross.

"When you're ready, Ray."

"Standby... go."

We kept low and rolled across to the wheels as planned. I got behind the port mainwheel and wrapped myself under the back of the wheels and stayed there for a breather.

Ray did the same on the starboard wheel. If anyone looked now all they would see were two wheel chocks, one in front of the tyres and one behind, with the rear ones gasping for air!

"Ok, Peter?"

"Yes... go."

I pulled the front chuck around the side of the wheel and positioned it behind the tyre. Then I rolled across the concrete to the nosewheel and did the same there. Ray chocked the back of other wheel then rolled across and joined me.

He stood up and stepped on the nosewheel tyre. The door to the aircraft was only two feet above him now, underneath the fuselage. He looked around quickly and saw the police Landover moving towards us.

"Peter," he whispered urgently,

"Get ready."

He leant across, slipped his key into the door lock and turned the recessed handle.

I leapt up, dragged the door down and pulled the ladder out. Ray was across and into the cockpit like greased lightning even before the door was half open.

He grabbed hold of the door closing lever and pushed it hard over to the closing position.

I could have killed him there and then on the spot. The door was closing fast, I was on the outside and the patrol was just turning into the dispersal from the perimeter track.

The Landover headlights were turning towards me.

Fear does wonderful things to the human body at times.

The body that I happened to be in at the time shot upwards like a rocket, without me knowing anything about it, grabbed hold of the top of the ladder and bent its legs forward about a micro second before the door hammered into its aluminium frame in the fuselage, with a solid sounding 'clunk'.

I lay there trembling, like the front wheels of my car.

"I knew you'd make it," Ray said to me, as he prised my petrified fingers off the top rung of the ladder.

"Just keep quiet like a good boy until they go away."

It had taken us only eight seconds to get into the cockpit but it took eight years off my life.

The patrol came into the dispersal and pointed the headlights towards the aircraft. We could hear one of the occupants get out and walk around the aircraft checking that nobody was hiding in the wheel bays.

The footsteps got louder as they came forwards to the door... and stopped right underneath it.

I could hear the handle being turned, and saw the opening levers moving in front of my eyes...

... and I was still lying on the door!

There was nothing I could do, I just prayed that the good Lord would excuse me for taking his name in vain.

The police patrolman tried the lever a couple more times then returned to the Landover, obviously satisfied, because we could hear them move off to another dispersal pan.

All was quiet now.

We had got away with it.

In the meantime, however I had sweated buckets.

Ray, cool as a cucumber, helped me up from the door. I was still shaking.

"What's your problem?" was his offhand remark,

"They couldn't have got in. I had my foot jammed solid against the door-closing lever. Nothing would have opened that door, not even a crow bar.

I couldn't tell you though as he would have heard me."

I decided not to strangle him as he might become useful later on in the trip.

We did nothing after that for two minutes. We just sat and looked around. If this wasn't the same aircraft that we were sitting in on Saturday afternoon, then it was a damn good likeness.

As the man said, "Don't ask questions, just look."

"Ok, let's get ready." I had recovered my composure.

We strapped in, and I checked that the necessary switches were in the 'ON' position.

Once the battery was switched on, all I had to do was press the four rapid-start buttons, push the throttles forward, take the hand brake off and we'd be away.

I checked my watch ... Five minutes to go.

* * *

The bang was muffled; it was more like a soft thump than a bang.

The Duty Electrical Engineer looked up and nearly died on the spot.

"Don't worry, Mr Robinson. Just pretend you're dead," said one of the black figures.

"Captain Ball, SAS. We've just captured your main electrical distribution building. Would you join your other staff in the bus outside please, nothing to worry about I assure you."

He picked up the telephone and dialled a number.

It rang for a second or so before being answered.

"Good morning Sir, Captain Ball, SAS patrol leader.

I would like to advise you that in two minutes time we will be switching off the main electrical power to the station to simulate a sabotage attack.

This is no hoax.

This telephone line will stay open as verification.

Most of the other lines are out of order as we have just captured the telephone exchange."

In the control tower, the routine continued unchanged.

"Awacs 06 an final approach Sir. Checking in on talkdown frequency."

They could see it now, five miles from touchdown, with its landing lights on, running in on the glide path.

So could Corporal Richard Barnard.

He had been sitting at that gun since eleven o clock, and was fed up to the back teeth.

These exercises were all right in theory, but when you were up half the night chilled to the marrow it was no joke.

He was lining the big Boeing up in his sights.

"Bang, bang, you're dead."

He could now mark up another 'kill' in his log book. You were only allowed one 'kill' for each approaching aircraft; and when you worked the night shift, they were few and far between.

He looked down at his radar monitor.

"Killed it at four miles."

Suddenly he was plunged into pitch blackness.

At the same time a series of irregular popping sounds, resembling sub machine guns firing, came from the bottom end of the airfield.

He heard shouting and engines revving, and the alert sirens blaring away.

A voice shouted in his earphones. "Intruder alert, intruder alert."

He looked across at the main airfield as the emergency lights flashed on, then off again.

The big Boeing was now only two miles away preparing to land.

"Awacs 06, this is the tower, emergency overshoot, runway light failure. Acknowledge please."

"Thank you tower, overshooting now."

The four engines increased their power, and the aircraft started to fly over the runway, climbing to a safe height so that it could turn downwind again for another landing.

"Battery on, Peter... Engine start... Now."

I hit the rapid start buttons, throttles forward, power rising, hand brake off... go...

... and we were moving within six seconds.

The runway was only one hundred yards away, and I knew that I could get there in time, turn on and get rolling down it just as the Awacs was in the final stages of its overshoot.

Its four landing lights would give me enough light to see the runway, for me to get airborne.

At least that was how we planned and rehearsed it.

What we did not have at rehearsals was the cold and miserable Corporal Richard Barnard sitting with his gun, fed up to the back teeth.

"Control tower to Gunsite Four, check the Sleaford road dispersal. Engine flames have been reported. Acknowledge"

Corporal Barnard looked across.

"Nothing observed tower, all clear."

"Can you see the display aircraft?"

"Negative... Wait a minute... Movement on the peritrack I think... Standby."

He looked hard. His eyes were watering in the wind, but he had been sitting there for over two hours now, and his night vision was as good as it could be.

Yes, it was there.

He could just see a dark lumbering shape, vaguely outlined in the Boeing's landing lights, turning onto the runway.

"Tower, Gunsite Four. The display Vulcan is on the runway and rolling for takeoff."

The Duty Controller checked with his binoculars.

"What is he doing?"

Suddenly, it dawned on him what the alert was all about... he went cold... if that was a terrorist hit squad...

He looked around him at the now useless telephone lines.

There was no way he could block the runway with any of his vehicles.

He had to stop that aircraft getting airborne, and there was any one way he could now do it.

He picked up the radio microphone to the guns.

"Gunsite Four. Emergency.

Operation Bandit, I repeat, Operation Bandit.

This is for real. Bandit on the runway.

Acknowledge."

Corporal Barnard knew what he had to do that night.

He had practised for this type of emergency at weekends, in the daylight, at aircraft approaching him.

Which most enemy aircraft tended to do; but this was alien to all that.

He didn't hang around though.

The gun that he was sitting at was the training weapon, loaded with blanks...

He ran across to Gunsite Three, pulled out the locking pins, the breech safety guards and the red lanyards.

The gun was facing the wrong way... Dammit.

He got hold of the hydraulic turn lever, and traversed to the left.

"Come on... Move, damn you... Move."

As it came slowly around, he looked along the runway.

The Vulcan was halfway down now, with the Boeing directly above it.

He couldn't have fired even if he'd had it directly in his sights.

Both aircraft would have been blasted out of the sky.

He would have to wait.

He was almost there... Come on gun... Move yourself...

He was lined up at last.

The Boeing turned left, to go downwind again for another landing... the beams from the landing lights swung around in the sky, like searchlights...

... and the Vulcan disappeared.

What did his squadron commander say to all newcomers?

"If you cannot see your target, aim somewhere in front of it and let it find your line of fire."

And that's just what Corporal Richard Barnard did that night.

He pressed the firing button, and immediately two barrels let fly with tracer and live rounds.

It was like a ribbon of white hot steel shooting across the airfield, but it was blind firing into darkness.

* * *

I had just lifted off... undercarriage up... perfect.

Fly straight ahead... a slight turn to the right... now put on the starboard injection fuel pump and press the engine igniters.

A two hundred foot long flame shot out behind the starboard engines, with very dramatic air explosions which sounded and looked dreadful.

Anybody seeing it would think that the aircraft had been hit and was in serious danger... which was the purpose of the exercise.

Unfortunately for us, Corporal Bardnard saw it as well, re-adjusted his aim, and the line of tracer shells started moving towards us.

This was NOT supposed to happen.

Ray was looking out with the rear looking camera on his VDU at all this.

"Peter, they're supposed to be using blanks.

We've got tracer and live rounds being thrown at us.

Let's get out of here fast before we get hit. Hard left... go."

I flicked the joystick to the left, but you can't move a heavy aircraft fast out of the way, even if shells are spraying towards you like water from a hosepipe.

We didn't get away with it.

I felt them hit underneath the aircraft, felt an explosion and saw flames on my left hand side followed by heavy rumblings and vibrations.

I now had flames underneath me on the port side, as well as the afterburner flames coming out of the starboard engines.

We must have been lit up like a Christmas tree; and I felt like the sacrificial turkey.

"Ray, I'm losing control.

I'm yawing all over the place.

Get ready to drop the external fuel tanks."

I could see Fulbeck airfield on the video screen now, so I tried to follow the plan.

Descend; keep the starboard afterburners on to simulate the fire as long as possible...

... not that I needed to...

Keep it going down, aim for the middle of the airfield...

... down, down, down; and I was there...

... nearly on schedule...

About a hundred feet over the aiming point.

I didn't want to jettison the tanks, but I had to. I was slewing sideways all over the sky.

They hit the grass to the south side of the runway.

My flames disappeared and the vibrations stopped.

Corporal Barnard had hit my port underwing fuel tank, at night, in the freezing cold, with me taking evasive actions.

Under normal circumstances I would have given him a medal there and then, but at the time I just wanted to get out of there as quickly as possible, so I followed the rehearsed procedure.

Afterburners off, throttles back, pull back on the joystick and ease the aircraft quietly up to a safe altitude... Gently does it...

And we disappeared once again into the black sky.

* * *

The explosion was the biggest in the area since the Humberside Flixborough disaster.

NIREX had done their job all right, only a lot keener than they needed to.

For the last week they had been stuffing bits of dismantled Vulcan aircraft into a big hole that they had dug in the centre of the airfield. Then they filled it full of fuel tanks brimming with aviation fuel.

The amount of explosives that they used could have demolished the Houses of Parliament.

Add to this the fuel that we dropped and you had a recipe for disaster:

The western half the village nearest the airfield disappeared immediately. Every dwelling to the west of the main Lincoln to Grantham road was blown to bits, in some cases not even the foundations remained.

Jack Morrily was no more.

His farm, his family, his beloved tractor and plough were hit by two flaming engines, part of a fuselage and tons of exploding fuel.

The public house disintegrated completely in a storm of bricks, roof tiles and flying glass then ended up spread all over the surrounding fields.

The rest of the houses, which survived the initial blast waves, were covered with high octane fuel, for about half a second, and then the whole village was consumed by fire.

The wind was from the south west that night, running up the valley formed by the Lincoln edge escarpment.

It fed the flames, by providing the oxygen necessary to assist combustion.

A firestorm developed, and a furious inferno raged uncontrollably throughout the night and most of the following day.

The reflection of the flames in the night sky were seen as far away as London.

It was worse than the Blitz.

Nobody in the village survived that dreadful night, not even the goldfish in the village pond.

It took the combined Fire and Rescue Services of Lincolnshire and Nottinghamshire three days of hot sickening work to get the fires and all the bodies out and when they had finished Fulbeck was merely a charcoal replica of its former self.

* * *

We didn't hear about any of this until we arrived at Gan.

All I knew at the time was a brightening of the sky that was all part of the great deception, as we went on our way to Rendezvous One, en-route for the Indian Ocean.

Shock has different effects on different people.

When they told us, I just sat down and cried.

That was the point when I wondered just what the hell we were all playing at.

Chapter 7. Typhoon & Concorde Services

I flew the aircraft as gently as I could and climbed up to about five thousand feet. The intention was to climb as high as possible, heading out towards the Atlantic to the south of Ireland, then fly south to the Azores.

That way we would be out of everybody's way, with minimal chance of being detected.

From the Azores we would fly across the Sahara Desert for our first rendezvous.

There was an emergency base there where we could land if we needed to, but the intention was to get to Gan in one long flight.

At the moment it felt as if we wouldn't even get out of Britain the way the aircraft was flying.

"Ray, send a message on the main computer to Gan control centre and ask what the hell they were up to back there.

This aircraft is flying like a pregnant duck.

We're not leaving these shores until we get it right."

"I'm ahead of you, pal. They're also getting the technical data from around the aircraft.

They can work out what the damage is, and tell us what to do about it.

They got us into this. They can get us out of it."

I knew what he meant.

We had both experienced the experts on the ground who officially criticised actions taken in the heat of the moment, in an aeroplane, by the aircrew under stressful conditions.

It's different when you're sitting in a quiet office with all the information in front of you in one thick file.

I can still see the report of my first major accident.

:THE DAMAGE COULD HAVE BEEN ALLEVIATED, IF THE CAPTAIN HAD CARRIED OUT THE CORRECT EMERGENCY PROCEDURES:

Never mind the fact that the poor co-pilot had half his face smashed in at the time, and that my right arm was broken, and that two engines were burning the wing off.

Two aircraft in the same piece of sky at the same time tend to cause a bit of damage to people and property when they hit each other, and all the experts could say about it was that I didn't turn the main fuel cocks off in time to reduce the fire.

Fat chance with a Cessna stuck in your wing.

I could see the reply to Ray's question regarding the live ammunition in the guns come up on the VDU.

:THE USE OF TRACER AND LIVE SHELLS WAS TO PROVIDE AN EFFECTIVE DISPLAY OF THEIR INTENTION TO DESTROY THE AIRCRAFT.

THE OPERATOR ON DUTY WAS SELECTED FOR HIS INEXPERIENCE AND POOR FIRING ABILITY:

Bully for them. If that was their worst guy, the rest deserve medals.

Next time, 'They' can come with us and have their heads resonated in the barrel.

"I wander who's side they're on, Peter. We could have done without that."

Just then the aircraft gave a lurch to the right.

My heart went into my boots.

An amber coloured warning light came on in front of me and a red flashing message appeared on the VDU.

:MAIN RUDDER FAILURE. STANDBY UNIT UNSERVICEABLE:

The emergency circuits were working all right and giving me warnings.

The aircraft was swinging gently from left to right as it flew through the air.

That's the trouble with a delta wing. Once it gets into a yawing motion it's difficult to control without the rudder. It gets worse and worse, and the aircraft has been known to alternatively swing each wing vertically into the air.

It's called Dutch Rolling. I was in for a hard time if it couldn't be repaired pretty damn quick

"Ray, I've lost the rudder completely. It's been soft and spongy for the last five minutes, but there's nothing there at all now."

The rudder bar was just flopping left and right under my feet, without any movement on the indicator in front of me.

The little picture of the flying controls should have told me that the rudder was moving, but it stayed vertically upright.

"Damn and blast.

I was expecting that.

The systems monitor shows no electrical power at all to the unit.

Those shells must have hit its electrical panel at the back of the aircraft. I suppose I'll have to go and have a look.

Dammit."

I was shocked at this outburst. It was most unlike him.

"You want to watch it Ray, it's cash in the swear box if you carry on like that."

I could have sworn I heard the chink of two coins going into his little plastic jar, which he had screwed onto the rear nav table to stop others pinching it.

"Joking apart Ray, you'd better go and have a look.

I can't get the other standby rudder power unit an either. It's kaput as well.

Take your hammer and belt it one will you?"

He sighed with despair and went aft to the bomb bay.

Immediately behind the rear navigation equipment was the nose wheel bay, and electrical control gear. By opening a pressure door in the rear bulkhead of the cabin he could crawl over the strengthened floor to the front end of the bomb bay compartments in the centre fuselage of the aircraft.

If the aircraft was a commercial airliner, these compartments would be full of fare paying passengers, but the cargo loaded later on would be much more sinister.

There were six of these down the main fuselage, each with a curved floor which rotated sideways to allow a space through which the bombs, or anything else, would drop.

We both had mental visions of Monsieur Jacques le Boustarde and his two big apes sitting in one of these 'cabins', quietly sipping their afternoon tea and nibbling their fairy cakes, only to find the floor shifting from underneath them.

Revenge is so sweet!

The front bomb bay compartment was about twenty feet long and the other five compartments about six feet.

If anything longer was needed, then the separating walls between them could be removed to form larger spaces.

Ray walked down the catwalk beside the bays to the rear of the fuselage. He was using a radio microphone so that he could describe any physical damage not picked up by the systems monitor.

At the rear of the bomb bay he crawled through a circular tunnel to where the rudder power units were positioned.

These were big powerful electrical hydraulic motors, which pushed the rudder into the airflow, to control the aircraft.

This was impossible to do by the pilot. There is not enough strength in a human being's leg muscle to do it.

It was a fairly simple emergency with few complications.

No rudder meant no control.

It would not be easy to turn the aircraft, particularly towards a runway, when you were about two or three hundred feet above the ground, with a strong crosswind crabbing you sideways in the direction of one of the biggest and hardest hangars you'd ever seen in your life!

You could get rather a nasty headache if you happened to hit it...

... which was why Ray was groping his way through the fuselage with his big hammer, to belt everything back into place again!

"How're you doing Ray?"

"Not too bad. Just make sure you stay in the air until I get back."

Poor chap. He couldn't wear his parachute. There wasn't room for both of them so he had to take it off before he went aft.

I could sense his concern, so I re assured him.

"Don't worry, pal. We are flying straight and level, and quite steady.

I'll tell you if we're going to hit the ground. You just get on with what you're doing."

He tended to worry a lot did our Ray!

"It's the fibre optic distribution panel Peter.

It's been hit through the middle by one of the shells.

There is no electrical power to the main rudder motor.

The second one has had the connecting rod knocked off, which is why it hasn't taken over automatically.

I can't repair the panel, but I can change over the rods.

It'll take me about twenty minutes, so fly like eggs, while I undo the bolts and get it connected up."

It all made sense now.

We would be all right when he changed over the connecting rods, to give me control from the standby rudder, but the panel would need replacing at Gan before the operation.

I keyed the information into the main communications computer to let Gan aware of the damage, and told them our immediate repair actions.

After that I just sat and watched the passing scenery, as poor old Ray sweated away at the back of the fuselage in the electrical compartment, getting more and more fed up with life.

The various roads were lined with sodium lights, the cars and other vehicles driving along, with their headlights stretched out in front of them.

Each town was different, in that the street lights produced differing patterns unlike the US of A where everything was in rectangular blocks.

I could see the two Severn bridges ahead of me, which would give me a nav check point until we could get the aircraft fully serviceable.

I could keep the aircraft wings level by very carefully moving the ailerons to counteract any swing produced by the crosswind.

Suddenly the rudder bars kicked in beneath my feet as the power unit came on line, the standby rudder warning light went out and the main rudder light went to amber as a warning sign.

"It takes a man to do a man's job," Ray said.

"You can play with your aeroplane now. I'm coming back for a rest and to cool off.

It's like a sauna down here, I've sweated buckets, so take it easy will you.

I've no intention of spreading myself all over the inside of this catwalk."

About ten minutes later I saw Ray's thumb up by my right shoulder.

He was back.

"Well Ray, my fine friend, you have a small task ahead of you."

There was a stunned silence.

I think he had visions of another walkabout to the depths of the aircraft again.

"OK, let's have it."

"You'll like this one.

Have a word with our controller at Gan, and ask them to work out how we are going to get to the middle of the Indian Ocean, with twenty percent of our fuel gone, thirty minutes behind time and about five hundred miles north of where we should be; whilst I test the systems and take this beast up to height."

I heard a few indistinct mutterings from behind me, about some people who just sat on their backsides giving all the orders, whilst others ran round in circles flogging themselves to death.

There appeared to be the odd expletive intermingling with The Queen's English as is taught at school, and the merry chink of coins various, going into a certain little container.

It didn't take long.

Change of plan.

We were under instructions to fly to Land's End at forty thousand feet, take up a southerly course, cruise climb to maximum operational height, ending up on two engines.

That way we would get maximum distance with the remaining fuel, and eventually link up with the refuelling aircraft two hundred miles east of Casablanca.

"Well, Ray, my fine friend, if this doesn't work we will spend a pleasant week down at the souk in Casablanca, whilst 'They' get this machine back into trim."

The front infra red camera picked up the hotel on the cliff top at Land's End. It was as clear as a bell on the screen.

The lights of the restaurant showed up brilliantly, and there was no difficulty in finding it.

The people at table five were having Nuits St George with their fish.

Most undignified! A nice white Vouvray would have been better.

I set the visual markers onto the south east corner of the building, pressed the key on the head up display and let the computer do all the work.

It was hard work this flying.

Decisions all the time...

The menu in the restaurant was making me peckish. I looked at my miserable rations; Chicken or beef sandwich. Which would it be?

"How are you doing Ray? Fancy a bit of chicken?"

My important decision had been made.

"On your bike," was his undignified reply.

* * *

It was ten minutes later before we saw them.

"We've got company."

"OK, feed them onto the port screen."

There were two aircraft. They had taken off from St Mawgan and were searching for us.

It was obvious from the traces that they were making an our VDU screens.

They looked like two dogs sniffing around for a bone, but they didn't stand a chance.

"Better help them out, Ray."

He switched on the radar homing device that would feed a signal to their screens, so that the crews could find us.

It was the last thing we wanted to do, but orders were orders.

The traces stopped sniffing.

They had found the scent!

"Closing in, seven o'clock, range twenty five miles, ten thousand feet below."

Like a pair of vultures they were, swooping in for the kill, and we were letting them do it.

It didn't take them long to find us, but they only saw us visually after they got on station.

One on the port wing, and the other to starboard; black and menacing with four missiles slung underneath.

It would have taken me some hectic flying to get away from that lot. They were making sure that we were out of the country all right.

"Got them, Ray?"

"Yes."

He could see the Typhoons out of the side windows.

"Tempting, isn't it?"

I couldn't suppress the grin. I knew what he meant.

It was like riding down the motorway, and having two-leather coated Hells Angels riding outboard on their brand new flash motorbikes...

... and you were the one with the turbocharged Harley Davidson with eight cylinders...

I looked down at the throttles, and mentally pushed them fully forward as I eased the control stick backwards.

It would have been like a Shuttle getting airborne.

But I could only dream.

They stayed there, glued to my wingtips for thirty minutes, as we flew south out of British airspace.

"Escort 32."

That was Cornish Radar calling them.

"Approaching the boundary now. Are you still visual?"

"Affirmative Cornwall. Good contact and heading outbound."

"Roger, return to base."

I looked at the Typhoon on the starboard wing and saw both of the crew looking at me.

It reminded me of my own flying days in the Royal Air Force... ninety percent boredom, ten percent panic... so I took hold of the little joy stick, flicked off the auto pilot, and rocked my wings...

I heard one of them call the other on the radio.

"Escort 34, this is Escort 32.

Close up for return to base."

That was for the benefit of the listening radar controllers, who were recording everything said on the frequency.

 "Roger, 32, closing up now."

They both moved inwards, and flew right on my wingtips.

I had switched the Vulcan's navigation lights on by this time, plus an optional extra that we had which made our silver surface glow in the pitch black.

They could both see me quite clearly now.

I gave a 'thumbs up' to each of them, which was returned, then pushed the stick forward.

Both Typhoons remained glued to those wingtips during the next few minutes.

It wasn't as good as the Red Arrows, but just as satisfying.

Where else could you see three deltas in very close formation?

We did three superb barrel rolls around the full moon, which was sitting low in the sky, completely clear of any clouds.

The old camaraderie, apparently, was still there.

It never dies.

I then took them down into a steep dive downwards, and pulled back on the stick.

The leader transmitted to the ground control base.

"Cornish Radar, Escort 32.

Target has cleared airspace, returning to base."

I pulled the stick further back, and the moon now disappeared under the Vulcan's nose.

At the top of the loop I held the aircraft inverted for at least ten seconds, and then pulled the stick back again.

The two Typhoons just continued on towards their base, inverted; whilst I continued the other half of the loop, back onto my original outbound heading.

They were gone.

Their job done, and once more we had the sky to ourselves.

At least we had now proved that the rudder power units worked. If they hadn't, we would have fallen out of the sky, and made a big splash somewhere in the British Channel.

During the transit Ray and Gan had worked out the revised flight plan.

It would need two refuellings, one in West Africa, and the other near the island of Socotra.

We needed to cruise climb and get as high as possible.

There would come a certain point when we would cut out number one engine as we got lighter; and then about an hour later cut out number four engine, eventually ending up on the two inboards - still climbing.

If we changed the course to cross over Southern Spain he calculated that we could just make the rendezvous in time.

We would re start the two engines at altitude, using the liquid hydrogen peroxide fuel injectors.

The alternative was to use the ground base which could blow our security.

"You've double checked the flight operation?" I asked Ray.

"Yes, with both computers."

The decision was made.

"OK, Ray, feed the data into the autopilot, then get your head down for a couple of hours. You could be busy in a couple of hours."

Once again he had beaten me to it.

All three autopilots linked together and took the aircraft out of my control, and within two minutes I heard a series of snores emanating from the rear of the cabin.

That lad could sleep anywhere!

* * *

We weren't the only ones flying south that night.

"British Airways Concorde Flight 245 to Casablanca is ready for boarding."

The early morning Concorde was on its milk run to Morocco.

The passengers filed through the terminal, only interested in getting to their seats so that they could get their heads down for a couple of hours sleep before landing.

Some of the keener ones were invited up front to see the flight deck. But Jacques le Boustarde was not interested in any of this.

He just wanted to sleep.

He checked his watch... 1.45am.

They had delayed the flight until he had arrived. The minor irritation in his plans was nothing to the rollocking those two idiots would receive next time he saw them.

He read his itinerary. Change at Casablanca and catch the North African Concorde Express direct to Addis Ababa, then Tristar to Gan.

He settled down into his seat and dozed off.

"Good morning, Sir."

He felt the hand on his shoulder. It was the stewardess with his drink.

He grunted and checked out of the window. He could see Gibraltar in the far distance, they were obviously near descent.

"We'll be landing in fifteen minutes, Sir. Would you like a coffee?"

He had a quick breakfast, checked his briefcase, and watched the passing scenery during descent and landing.

It was hot in the terminal, even at that time in the morning.

Passport and visa control eventually cleared him for his connection, and he joined the milling throng in the passenger lounge.

This was the long leg of his journey and the sooner it was over the better. He put on his seat belt and read the latest magazine.

The service was good. He had another breakfast and listened to the crew's descriptive comments about the scenery.

The passengers were keen. For some of them it was their first flight, and at their present altitude they could see for miles.

"Ladies and Gentlemen," it was the Captain's voice this time,

"We have just reached fifty five thousand feet, and if you look over to your right you can see Mount Tahat, which is about nine thousand feet in height.

There is no danger in hitting it.

Thank you."

The usual outburst of laughter soon died down after a few seconds.

"Excuse me Sir, would you like to visit the flight deck and meet the crew.

There is a party just leaving."

Le Boustarde looked up.

It was the young Moroccan stewardess smiling sweetly at him.

"Yes, of course, thank you very much."

"If you follow me, Sir, I can introduce you to the Captain."

They made their way forward. He had seen the flight deck before so he knew what to expect.

The Captain of the aircraft sat in the left hand seat, the Second Pilot to the right, and behind him the Flight Engineer.

The aircraft was on auto pilot, which allowed the crew to converse without too much concentration on the flying.

"We are on course, and on schedule Monsieur le Boustarde." He checked his watch.

"Thank you Captain. I'll just sit quietly until all is complete."

* * *

I saw the condensation trail from fifty miles away.

It was like a silver thread across the sky.

"Can you take it now, Ray, and I'll make the coffee."

He had been getting his head down for an hour or so whilst I flew the first leg, so there were a few unenthusiastic grunts from him as we changed over!

It was a relief to get out of the seat and stretch my legs out on the bunk.

"I'll follow the trail for a while on autopilot whilst we check our position.

I've got him on the TV camera about ninety miles ahead."

Ray was now in charge.

I was going to relax and leave him to it.

We curved round onto an easterly heading, with the white trail now straight ahead of us.

We saw the Concorde five minutes later, a tiny white triangle far ahead.

"He's on schedule, Ray."

We were about ten thousand feet above him and gaining.

We could see Mount Tahat in the distance.

"Hydrogen peroxide on, starting outboard engines."

We could both feel the rumbling through the airframe, and see the needles rising as the engines started up again.

"All four running, taking over manual control.

I'll follow the trail for a while until I get the feel of the aircraft."

It was quite sensible because he hadn't flown it yet, so he didn't know how it would respond to his movements on the little joystick.

Up until now he had only been playing 'video games' in our static simulator.

Ray switched the autopilot out, pulled the throttles back, and started a smooth descent towards the Concorde.

The tiny triangle increased in size as we closed up to within a mile behind. Ray eased the throttles forward slowly and it wasn't very long before he had the Concorde's wingspan filling the full width of his centre cockpit window.

He held it there steady as a rock for a full minute.

It was perfect.

He was not playing games any more.

He was flying... and he was good.

The four square nacelles were immediately above us.

It was just as well we were not supersonic. We would have been blown out of the sky with all that power.

Ray eased slowly forward until he was underneath the end point of the fuselage.

A panel opened up just forward of the rear cargo bay access hatch, and a long flexible hose trailed out, with a long narrow funnel at the end.

It was about fifty feet above us.

Ray flew the Vulcan up and moved slowly forwards, until the refuelling probe was pointing towards the outer lips of the funnel.

He held it there for a second or two, then very gently eased forward and inserted the tip of the probe slowly into the circular valve at the centre of the funnel.

When he was properly connected the VDU screen turned green in front of him.

He had got the probe in first time. We held that position for about fifteen minutes, as I checked that all the tanks were filled.

We would need all the fuel we could carry if we were to get to the second rendezvous.

"Ok, Ray.

Full up.

You can clear away now."

Ray had been flying 'hands on' during the whole sequence, and had kept the probe locked deeply into the funnel.

It was essential to keep a forward positive pressure all the time, otherwise it could slip out with disastrous consequences. There would have been fuel spraying out all over the place.

This was something the computers could not yet achieve. It still needed the pilot to keep control.

He was reaching the critical point in the whole operation now.

He had noticed the hose begin to whiplash in front of him. If it became uncontrollable it could bend the probe or even knock it off.

That had happened to one of the aircraft during the Falklands campaign.

The hose oscillations became wilder, and were increasing in ferocity as he reduced the forward pressure. He had to pull away sharply otherwise there could be serious damage to the aircraft.

He pulled back on the throttles and withdrew cleanly. The only leakage was a slight spurt of fuel which splattered over the windscreen in front of his face before the funnel valve closed tightly.

It could have been worse. He had often had his front window smothered with fuel on previous withdrawals, when he was younger and more inexperienced.

The VDU changed to amber in front of him, as the hose was reeled into the bay underneath the Concorde.

The funnel disappeared, the panel closed and the amber colour changed to green.

The first flight refuelling sequence was completely satisfactory to both agencies.

The Vulcan was full up now, and the Concorde had lost a little bit of her ability to go all the way to Addis Ababa.

We slowed down and let the distance increase between us. When Concorde was about a mile ahead Ray pushed forward with the throttles, and we climbed up to a higher altitude to continue.

"It's been quite a while since I did that" he remarked.

I could see now why they'd picked him. It was the first time he'd had his hands on that aircraft, and within ten minutes it was doing everything he asked.

I bet he could break a few girl's hearts on the ground!

He was definitely a smooth operator.

I could visualise them swooning with expectation of an evening's delight!

"I'm going to get my head down while you play with your new aeroplane. Give me a call before descent."

It had been a long day since we started off from Waddington.

It felt like a week.

I was asleep within five minutes.

* * *

The Concorde engineer checked the fuel gauges.

"Transfer complete, Captain."

"Thank you," he replied, and turned round in his seat.

Le Boustarde nodded then returned to the passenger lounge.

He was just sitting down when the announcement came over the speaker.

"Ladies and Gentlemen, this is the Captain speaking. I regret that we have a small problem with one of our engines, and will not be able to continue to Addis Ababa.

We shall return to Casablanca and transfer you to our other aircraft."

Suitable apologies followed, plus free food and drinks for the rest of the return flight, and the passengers were eventually satisfied.

Le Boustarde sipped his fourteen year old malt whisky and looked at the desert below.

It was hostile, barren and stretched for miles in all directions. A wilderness of red hot sand and rock in which only the Bedouin could survive.

"If they had missed us," he surmised, "nobody would have missed them, and they would have made a big beautiful hole in that desert.

They wouldn't have been found for years."

He let out a sigh.

"It would have been a pity about the aircraft though."

Chapter 8. Hydrofoil Tanker Services

Captain Olaf Petersen was the chief tanker captain for BP (TANKERS) Plc, a shipping and transportation company set up within the BP consortium of companies, privatised many years ago by the British Government.

He had been a seaman all his working life, from the age of twelve when he was a young boy on his father's fishing trawler, sailing out of Bergen in Norway with the North Atlantic fishing fleet.

His seamanship included experience of Arctic conditions, whaling, deep sea fishing, and North Sea oil rig tendering within the Norwegian sector of the continental shelf oil field. He had been head hunted by BP twenty years ago, and had remained in that organisation ever since.

His knowledge of marine technology ranged further than sea captaincy required, and resulted in him receiving high accolade from the present Board of Directors and shareholders of the company.

It was his innovation and persistence that had resulted in the latest and most modern design of the submersible hydrofoil oil tanker, in use by the UN forces in operation within the Terrorist War zone of the Persian Gulf.

He was now sitting in his seat in the operations control room of the flagship, 'The Pride of BP Enterprise', en route from the Seychelles in the Indian Ocean to Kuwait, for another load of liquid petroleum gas and high octane gasoline.

These were the most dangerous items to transport down the Gulf at the present moment.

They produced a very high financial reward, and as BP were the only tanker operators capable of carrying out this work, it was 'write your own sales cheque time' until somebody else obtained the Petersen technology.

"What's our position please, Number One?"

His first officer checked the inertial navigation system in front of him.

"Five hundred and sixty miles east of Socotra island Captain, heading and speed good for the Gulf of Arabia."

He checked the wind speed and direction on the VDU screen in front of him.

It was reading twenty five knots blowing directly towards the tanker.

"Maintain speed and heading directly into the wind Number One, adjust for any drift."

"Aye, aye sir," the first officer replied, and concentrated on his computerised controls in front of him.

The other members of the crew included the communications officer and the ship's engineer. Each had an appropriate computer in front of them, applicable to their own sphere of interest.

They sat alongside each other, allowing the most efficient form of communication between them.

Captain Petersen had insisted that in a war situation, any member of the bridge crew must be capable of taking overall command if events warranted it.

So far, his good advice had not been required; and they had now been together for three years.

The last member of the crew, 'Moggy', the ship's cat, was curled up asleep in her cat box, with her little orange life-jacket on, just in case of a rapid departure.

They had all teamed up together after the launch at the Barrow in Furness shipyard on the Cumbrian coast.

The Poseidon submarine contract had been temporarily postponed during the tanker's construction and sea trials period, and afterwards for the duration of the building of the rest of the present BP fleet.

Theirs were the only tankers in the world immune to Air to Ship missile attacks and direct bombing.

Their sonar equipment could detect sea mines, and their manoeuvrability was such that immediate evasion from the torpedo mines resting on the sea bottom could be successfully achieved.

In all the hundreds of operations from Kuwait, not one loss had been registered.

This was all as a direct result of a previous attack on Captain Peterson and his colleagues some years previously:

They had been in a convoy from Bahrain to Kuwait that day, under the protection of a light cruiser, two frigates and a glass reinforced plastic minesweeper-mine hunter, which swept a channel through the minefield for them.

They reached the refinery terminal safely but it was on the return trip when they got hit.

He was captain of the ultra large crude carrier, 'BP Global Carrier' at the time, and was sailing as the second ship in convoy, behind the sister ship, 'BP North Sea'.

Behind him were two other BP tankers, and a Japanese LPG tanker, registered in London by their British based company the previous week.

It was now called 'Afternoon Sun', and was very shortly to become one.

* * *

"Estimating aircraft rendezvous in twenty minutes, Captain."

Olaf Petersen looked up suddenly from his reminiscing.

"Thank you, Number One. Contact the aircraft on the computer.

Advise them position, heading and speed. Carry out a computer link-up as soon as possible."

"Aye, aye, sir."

They had received an e-mail a few hours earlier, advising them to prepare for an emergency refuelling at short notice; they were now in contact with the aircraft, and were adjusting their course and speed for the landing.

* * *

In 2005, his convoy had set off at midday in line astern.

The protection vessels sailed up and down the flanks, at action stations, searching for incoming hostiles both in the air and underwater.

The BP convoy comprised of two ULCCs each with nine hundred thousand tonnes displacement weight, and two VLCCs each with two hundred and fifty thousand tonnes.

It represented a considerable amount of capital investment, and about a hundred and fifty million pounds worth of petroleum products.

The Japanese tanker was the latest version, and three quarter million tonnes of modern technology on its maiden voyage.

Captain Petersen had been on the rear bridge during departure from Kuwait, supervising the clearance from the deepwater offshore terminal; but was now on duty in the forward control room in the reinforced bow section, for the passage down the Gulf.

"Number One to Captain. Ship on station at convoy speed."

"Thank you Number One, maintain position."

He leant over the war operations computer screen, and surveyed the immediate area.

The other four blips had shown up clearly, with the minesweeper about three miles ahead on its first sweep.

The cruiser was on the starboard flank, with the two frigates to port, one at the front of the convoy and the other at the rear.

The tanker ahead could just be seen through the haze and shimmering atmosphere.

He checked it with his binoculars, through the armoured glass set in the front bulkhead of the control room positioned low on the deck.

It was turning a couple of points to starboard under the instructions from the cruiser, which he could hear on the UHF receiver.

"BP global Carrier, next heading one one zero degrees. Acknowledge please."

"Roger, convoy leader."

That was Number One, reporting from the rear bridge.

Number One would carry out the routine manoeuvres as instructed by the cruiser, until the Bahrain check point, when he would hand over his little bit of authority back to Captain Petersen.

It was a standard operating procedure to have two control rooms on the Gulf ships, in case one of them got hit. At least there would be the chance that the other one could maintain control of the vessel in extreme emergency conditions.

The journey was uneventful, until two fifty five that afternoon.

There was an immediate message from the RADAR operator on the ship's tannoy system.

:Attention. Attention. Inbound missiles coming from the starboard side and dead ahead:

He saw a missile strike the port side of the rear bridge.

Ten seconds later he saw a second missile fly across the mid section of his ship, and hit the dead centre of the rear bridge.

The crew didn't stand a chance.

The whole superstructure was now a mass of flames.

A second pair of missiles shot straight across the mid-section of his tanker, and carried on across the flat sea.

The next pair of Exocets came from behind the tanker, and hit the rear bridge again.

Captain Petersen was in shock, and his brain was to record these missiles strikes for posterity.

The other two BP tankers behind his ship didn't last long.

They were small game compared to the big boys which the aircraft had demolished so far.

Within five minutes they were on fire from bow to stern.

The crude oil poured out from the burning tanks.

The surface of the sea was on fire between all three tankers, and there was no way anyone could have survived that inferno.

The only remaining vessel was the Japanese tanker.

The biggest in the world, and bulging with liquid petroleum gas.

The fireworks finale was about to begin.

Twelve aircraft formed up in waves of 'finger four', and circled round the tanker at a radius of about five miles until they were ready:

And when they hit it, they hit it hard.

There were four Exocets to each wave, and as the aircraft flew in, all were released at the same time.

The tanker blew up after the first four missiles hit it with an enormous explosion.

There was nothing left except an enormous spray of metal plates and bits and pieces of ship flying in all directions, with a huge ball of white hot fire at the centre.

The other eight missiles in two waves of four were not required.

They flew straight through the smoke, came out the other side, and flew off across the sea in similar fashion to the missiles that had flown across the midsection of his ship.

* * *

"The aircraft is approaching the descent point Captain.

The computers are linked up, and everything is satisfactory.

Gan control has given the go ahead for the refuelling.

Socotra Island is standing by for any emergencies."

"Thank you, Number One.

Check all engines and equipment, and advise the aircraft serviceable before it descends."

"Aye, aye, Sir."

They continued checking the tanker for the refuelling.

* * *

He remembered how some of the missiles flew into the pall of smoke, and hit parts of the superstructure, but he also remembered a number of more important facts.

There were those that flew straight through the smoke and disappeared into the sea.

There was the one that flew over him, straight through the smoke from the burning bridge of his own tanker, and disappeared; and there was the other one that shot across his sinking rear section, and hit the tanker behind.

None of them had hit him.

Why didn't they?

He had been on a fully laden tanker at the time, ready to be blown sky high, but they had flown right over him.

... They could not have seen the middle section of his ship.

... They could not have picked up the hull which was low in the water.

... They were obviously aiming for the ship's superstructure.

It was beginning to dawn on him.

The missiles were all flying at a pre-set altitude, and they were aiming for vertical sections of steel represented by bridges and upper parts of vessels.

They had not seen the hull of his ship, which was lying very low in the water.

He had spoken to James Jefferson, the BP main designer, told him what he had seen, and made a few suggestions.

It took two weeks to design the new Petersen tanker on paper, then another week to make up the scale model for testing at the Teddington ship tanks.

When the bugs were ironed out of the system, a tenth scale working version was constructed and tested on Coniston Water in the lake District.

Within three months of its original conception the Board of Directors of BP had given approval, and the first of the Petersen tankers was built at the Barrow in Furness shipyard.

* * *

"All systems satisfactory Captain.

The aircraft has commenced descent.

We estimate visual contact in fifteen minutes."

Captain Petersen got up and checked the weather radar and the latest satellite reports.

"Make the heading zero one zero degrees, and test both computers with a surface speed of fifty five knots.

That will give us a bit in hand if it's needed."

He walked across the operations room of his flagship and looked down at the cat.

"Come on, Moggy, it's time for a walk."

The feline expended about a micro-joule of energy, by lifting a disinterested eyelid in his direction and gave a bored yawn.

Her job was to rid the tanker of little brown furry jobs, not go for walks.

She snuggled deeper into her cushion and carried on snoozing.

Olaf picked her up and carried her to his seat. They had found her in the alleyways of Muscat and she went everywhere with them.

The ritual was the same every time.

She always played hard to get. Typical woman!

She purred away contentedly as he stroked her chin.

"The speed and heading checks OK with the aircraft computer, Captain.

The main Gan computer has verified. All engines are good.

Do you want to lift the tanker up onto the hydrofoils now Sir?"

"Yes please Number One. Get it all ready for them.

I'll check with Gan control for any last hitches."

* * *

The tests had been conclusive.

The full scale version had passed all sea trials under secrecy, including a direct bombing raid by Tornadoes, and a double Exocet strike aiming straight at it.

Captain Petersen was so confident about his tanker that he put himself in charge of the vessel during those attacks, and nobody could find him to hit him.

Which was just as well otherwise he wouldn't be here now!

They didn't find him, because when they tried to hit him, he was under water.

His tanker was a rectangular box, one hundred and twenty metres in length, thirty five metres in width and ten metres in depth.

It was constructed in the form of a sandwich, with steel plates as the bread, and a fireproof glass reinforced plastic mixture with lava extrusion as the filler.

This compressed foam was light, strong, and could withstand the direct impact of a five hundred pound bomb, should one have the misfortune to meet one coming vertically down towards you!

The power came from diesel engines mounted at each of the four corners of the box, the shafts protruding vertically downwards from underneath the vessel.

These were coupled to the propellers via rotating gears, and a full three hundred and sixty degree mounting, allowing the four propellers to move about in any direction, forwards, aft or sideways.

It looked like the top of a hovercraft, lying upside down in the water. The craft could turn around in a circle by angling the propellers in appropriate directions.

The front of the box was flat, and the control room section was bolted onto the box at this point.

This was shaped like a triangular wedge of cheese, and when it was in position, the top side of the wedge was flush with the top of the tanker, giving an overall top length of one hundred and forty metres from tip to stern.

The underside of the wedge formed an angle of thirty five degrees with the surface of the water.

Within the tanker were buoyancy chambers that allowed the whole vessel to sink low in the water with a full load of fuel.

The chambers could be adjusted to allow the topside of the box to be about a metre above the water line.

When the four propellers pushed the vessel forwards, the wedge forced upwards against the water, and the whole box tended to rise. At this point the buoyancy tanks were re adjusted.

More water ballast was taken on board, and at the designated cruising speed the tanker sank to a point where the top surface was just skimming the surface of the sea.

Underneath the box were five sets of hydrofoils stretching right across the width of the tanker.

Each set comprised of seven separate wings, all independent from each other, which could freely rotate vertically ninety degrees up or down.

In the horizontal position they could raise or lower the vessel in the water, and if all wings were vertical they acted as sea brakes.

The tanker could turn and stop on a sixpence if necessary, and could dive to fifty feet, level off and travel underwater like a submarine for a limited period of time.

It could take a load of fuel in the region of fifty thousand tonnes.

There were two small narrow conning towers on the control section, which remained above water under normal cruise conditions.

These had the air snorkels and communication sensors.

Navigation was done by GPS, and communications via the UN-intranet.

It was perfect for transits in the Persian Gulf Terrorist War Zone. The mines didn't bother it at all.

The sensing equipment picked them up, and the tanker submarine skirted them with ease as it either 'flew' around them on the hydrofoils or the whole vessel could dive under the water if necessary.

The major advantage was that once outside the Gulf and in relatively safe waters they could link up like a train to form a supertanker of up to five units in line, clamped together with hydraulic clamps, nose to stern.

With the buoyancy tanks blown, and riding up in the water, the front unit could pull all the others to the required destination.

When there was more than one destination they could detach, and each one which could sail into port independently.

Deep water anchorages were no longer required and BP were now on their way to writing their own income cheques, and virtually declaring any profit they wished to suit their own circumstances.

* * *

"Aircraft range is now fifty miles dead astern.

Our speed and heading as required Captain."

"Very Good Number One.

Advise the aircraft that we are ready"

There was another advantage in his tanker. When they were returning empty to the Gulf of Arabia before entering the Strait Of Hormuz, they could ride high in the water.

The wedge had been designed at thirty five degrees because the trials at the Teddington tanks had found that the water flowed evenly with minimum resistance under the base of each box at that angle.

With an empty tanker it offered the minimum water resistance as it travelled forwards.

When the hydrofoils were extended downwards underneath the vessel at this point, the tanker lifted up onto the five sets of wings and the resistance decreased significantly.

With a power setting of about eighty percent of full power available from all twenty diesel units in the five coupled tankers, the supertanker could transit across the ocean at a speed approaching sixty knots.

The hydrofoil wings were controlled by the computer in the forward control room, in which Captain Petersen was now sitting with his crew and the ship's cat.

The complete structure from front to rear measured seven hundred metres of flat surface, controlled by computer from gyroscopes set in the centre of each tanker, and it was travelling across a dead flat sea at a speed of fifty five knots into a steady wind of twenty five knots.

The relative wind speed over the top surface of the tanker was on average between eighty and eighty five knots.

"Aircraft now five miles dead astern Captain.

Computers are linked. All satisfactory."

"Thank you Number One.

Advise the aircraft captain that he is clear to land."

"Aye, aye, Sir."

* * *

He clicked 'OK'...

... And the screen changed to green on my flight instrument VDU.

... And I flew very low and very slow, nose up to the sky, across the flat sea towards his tanker, for landing and refuelling.

Chapter 9. Tankerland

To understand how the aircraft landed it was important to know how the delta wing worked. The Vulcan, Concorde and latest NASA Shuttle all used the same technique. There was a small problem that had to be overcome on landing which other aeroplanes did not have.

At slow speeds, as on landing, the angle at which the air attacks the wings of an aircraft must be increased to maintain the required lift. At a large angle, approximately fifteen degrees, the wings will create turbulence, stall and the aircraft will fall out of the sky.

Sensible people had recognised this important factor and it had been decided by early aviators since Pontius was a pilot that they would fly towards a runway above this stalling speed.

One big advantage of the delta wing which the Vulcan had, was that it didn't stall until much lower speeds than a normal wing, therefore the aeroplane could approach much slower than would be required with a normal aircraft.

There was only one major problem that had to be overcome. The wing was at such a high angle of attack at the landing speed that the drag of this 'tennis court' through the air tended to slow the aircraft down very quickly and drop it rapidly towards the very hard ground beneath it. The only way to overcome this on our aircraft was to use the engines at a higher percentage of power than normal to keep it in the air.

The primary airbrakes were used to stop the aircraft accelerating in speed and at the last moment the secondary airbrakes were pushed out into the airflow, then the aircraft would sink gracefully onto the runway with a gentle puff of smoke from the tyres... or so it said in the manual!

On this particular approach we had to fly at a speed lower than the aircraft's, 'stalling speed' at a height of fifty feet above the water.

And that's why I hate keen and enthusiastic people at times!

I levelled off at about fifty miles from the tanker and flew towards it at a height of around two thousand feet. Ray kept contact with the control room as I manoeuvred into a position about twenty miles behind it. I would then think about going lower down. But not before.

The main sensor would be the camera in the nose of the aircraft. At the touchdown point on the first of the five tankers were two strobe lasers pointing towards us. I would be able to see them as well and it would give me, the mere human pilot of the machine, a landing reference point. My other reference was the 'running rabbit' down the centre of the complete structure.

The centre line of the tanker had a set of lights, which were switched on and off alternatively. The end product was a single light, which started at this end of the 'runway' and ran up the centre to the far end before returning again.

The tanker computer fed the wind speed and tanker speed into our computer and the distance from the touchdown line was calculated from the two strobe lasers. All I had to do was sit and watch... then do the last bit!

Ray came up the front for a quick look around.

"When you're ready you can set it up in the final landing mode then we can get down and have a cup of tea."

He looked at me.

I must have looked really 'keen'!

"Go on. Down you go," he said as he pointed a finger downwards.

"On your bike," I said as I pointed two upwards.

The first part of the approach was to be done by me. I had to be at a point twenty miles behind the tanker at a height of one hundred feet above the sea, flying ten knots above 'stalling' speed. When all was well I had to descend very slowly to around fifty feet and gradually reduce speed until we dropped out of the sky. The first task was no problem but the second gave me the willies all right. I did not fancy it one bit.

I made sure that my right hand held the joystick quite firmly and my left hand on those throttles and afterburners for the fastest climb in Christendom. I also had a finger on the airbrake 'IN' switch and another on the undercarriage 'UP' switch. I could have done with a few more hands to play with the ejector seat buttons!

I was now down at the correct height flying at one hundred and thirty five knots. We would fall out of the sky at a hundred and twenty five.

"Undercarriage down Ray."

He pressed a key on the computer and I heard the rumbling as it travelled downwards and locked into place. I pushed the throttles forward slightly to maintain the speed.

"You're lined up now Peter.

OK for the computer?"

I took a final look around before committing myself. The speed was exactly as I wanted it. The tanker was seven miles ahead. The height was sixty feet above the water.

The angle of attack was high and the nose of the aircraft was pointing about thirty degrees up into the air. Any more than that and we would go down into the sea like a brick.

"OK Ray, computer on now."

I felt a slight tremor on the controls as the programme took effect. I could feel the nose being pulled back very slowly as the angle increased and felt the throttle tremble under my left hand.

The VDU showed the increase in the angle of the airbrakes as they increased the drag in the airflow.

The throttles moved forward to increase the power of the four engines each of which pushed the aircraft upwards to counteract the fall caused by the drag and the slower speed.

I sweated buckets!

The same procedure repeated itself and slowly the airspeed reduced, the angle of attack increased and eventually it was pointing up at an angle of thirty-five degrees at one hundred and twenty five knots; with the engines at about eighty five percent of their full power, and the airbrake plates at the maximum drag angle.

The aircraft then very slowly descended towards the sea.

I sweated more buckets!

I could feel my hands beginning to twitch. It took all my efforts not to ram the throttles forward and get the hell out of it.

I was just about to do so when I felt the burbling which we had been told to expect.

The aircraft had settled, in this case with the nose probe at a height of seventy five feet above the sea, the centre point of the aircraft at a height of fifty feet and what was more important, the full stretch of the rear of the delta wing twenty five feet above the water with the angle of attack at thirty seven degrees.

The air was being compressed as it flowed underneath the aircraft and because the surface of the water was so close, it was acting as a cushion for the flat under-surface to rest on like a hovercraft, or a flat piece of paper being pushed across a smooth table surface.

The Farnborough scientists had predicted this in the wind tunnel and were insistent that the 'ground effect' would support the aircraft at this speed in similar fashion to the Surface Effect Ships that were on trial with the Royal Naval authorities in the Southern Atlantic.

I am very pleased to report that they were correct.

In this fashion we continued forwards under the control of the main computer and the flight computer to the five-mile point. This was a major decision point.

If the tanker parameters were within the safety limits we would be given clearance for landing. If not, I would push the throttles forward, select the airbrakes in and bring the undercarriage up and try again.

I saw the screen flash green in front of me and Ray acknowledged.

"Enterprise, this is Zero One. Landing affirmative."

I could see the tanker ahead quite clearly now. The strobes were clear and distinct. The running rabbit was lined up exactly on the nose.

The flat surface of the tanker was riding smoothly on the hydrofoils. It was just like approaching a runway in a small aircraft at forty-five knots, which was lower than some of them actually do.

The mathematics of our approach worked out that we were landing on a six thousand feet concrete runway at our normal speed, which was quite feasible.

I was beginning to feel a lot more confident now.

Perhaps a shade overconfident as it turned out!

It was smooth all the way to the flare out point. This was at about three hundred feet behind the touchdown point on the tanker. I could see the touchdown line quite clearly across the deck.

A number of simultaneous actions had to take place for the aircraft to land correctly:

I had to push the throttles fully forward with my left hand and the joystick with my right...

The computer would push the secondary airbrakes out to kill the speed as quickly as possible and activate the reverse thrust hydraulic jacks...

These would push flat steel plates into the jet outlets of all four engines and deflect the airflow above and below the wings to produce a forward jet air flow...

It tended to force the aircraft backwards, and at the same time removed the thrust pushing the aircraft forwards...

The computer would control everything.

All I had to do was follow the instructions on the screen in front of me as if I were playing a game of space invaders at home!

At the decision point I saw the deck lined up dead ahead of me.

The throttles moved fully forward rapidly, the joystick was pushed fully forward and I felt the back of the Vulcan rise as the airflow hit the elevators.

The nose dropped to the horizontal position and the aircraft carried on in that attitude towards the tanker deck. I felt the reverse thrust bite as the plates were forced into the jets and heard the secondary airbrakes hammering into the airflow - and I could still see water between me and the tanker.

I must have been mad to agree to this.

Only a raving lunatic would carry out such a ridiculous action.

I just gaped open mouthed as the Vulcan dropped like a stone and, carried forward under its remaining momentum, thumped onto the deck of the first tanker like a lump of concrete on solid wooden wheels.

At the same time as it 'arrived', the reverse thrust had built to maximum forward power to offer the aircraft its greatest braking effect when it was most needed; the first ten seconds of landing to kill off most of the kinetic energy.

I pushed as hard as I could on my foot brakes in the rudder pedals under the balls of each boot.

I virtually stood on them to apply the brakes an each main wheel as hard as possible.

As the aircraft ran over the deck of the second tanker, the nose wheel ran over an arrester wire lying flat on the deck. Normally this would have been used for aircraft with arrester hooks.

The two arrester wires outboard of this centre wire were in the 'UP' position, to catch the struts of each main wheel. The aircraft engaged these at a speed relative to the tanker of forty knots.

I had felt the rudder slewing to the left as I pushed the throttles forward for the reverse thrust at the very beginning of the landing, and now it became more pronounced.

The nose of the aircraft suddenly started to turn towards the right, and we began to crab sideways up the length of the deck.

Something was wrong, but all the indications were correct.

The port undercarriage was leading at this point, and it hit the second set of cables slightly before the starboard, and set a sideways oscillation in motion.

All I could see in front of me was the deck of the tanker swinging from side to side, as the aircraft oscillations got wilder and wilder.

The speed slowed down, but not fast enough to stop us as predicted.

As we travelled sideways over the fifth tanker it was obvious to even me in my panic ridden gritted teeth state that Davy Jones was in for a couple of visitors.

The nose was pointing out towards the side of the tanker, the speed was about fifteen knots, when it should have been around five, and we only had about three hundred feet of surface left.

The last obstruction I saw was a tennis court net affair, stretched across the deck about two hundred feet from the lip of the tanker. It was made of reinforced nylon webbing and was designed to act as a final barrier to unfortunates such as ourselves.

The nose wheel and the port main wheel hammered into it at roughly the same time.

I felt myself being pushed forwards into my seat straps and hoped it would work.

No chance.

We slowed down all right but not sufficiently enough.

I was sitting about thirty feet in front of the nose wheel, travelling sideways, and I saw the end of the deck coming towards me.

The nose of the aircraft went slowly over it and I was following in very slow motion!

* * *

If you want to know what it was like put yourself in your brand new SAAB 990 Turbo, switch off the engine and coast into your garage.

Your servo-brakes won't work, because the engine has stopped, and you can see the wall of the garage ahead of you - but you can't stop in time.

You are slowing down, but eventually you are going to hit the wall at about five miles per hour.

If you cannot imagine that, then pretend you are watching your good lady wife do it after her first driving lesson, and you can only watch, with tears in your eyes, as your precious car crumples its lovely shiny bonnet on the rough concrete block wall.

Well, that's how I felt at the time and there was nothing I could do about it.

* * *

I was right over the edge of the deck when we hit something hard.

If I had been wearing false teeth they would have shot forward and clattered in fear on the instrument panel ahead of me. As it was, they were doing that quite nicely in my gums at the time.

I felt another bone crunching thud and I felt the nose of the aircraft suddenly dip downwards and slowly, very, very slowly, tip downwards towards the surface of the water.

I looked down underneath me and saw the water racing backwards at about seventy miles an hour and disappear under the front wedge of the tanker.

The port wing was tipping over the edge, and I could see the pitot tube breaking the white horses on the top of the waves.

A few more seconds and the top surface of the wing would be under water, and that would be it.

I just sat there… and suddenly felt very, very sick.

* * *

The tanker crew knew something was going to happen even before we did.

About two seconds before I pushed the throttles and joystick forward a loud bell rang on the front of the computer panel.

Olaf Petersen looked up rapidly and saw a flashing 'WINDSPEED' warning notice on the computer screen.

Underneath was another notice that said 'OUT OF LIMITS'.

He didn't stop to think.

He pressed the abort button on the panel in front of him.

This would turn both the screens in front of him, and the one in the aircraft, from normal black and white to red.

The pilot could then make the decision to fly off...

but it changed to green!

"Damn. The computer has accepted the aircraft.

Check the wind speed and direction Number One. I want to know fast."

It came immediately.

It was the first thing that he had looked at.

"It's shifted twenty degrees to starboard Captain, and dropped five knots. We must have hit a squall or a severe weather front for that to happen.

There's nothing on radar to indicate anything."

They watched the aircraft land on the deck, on the picture from the TV cameras on both of the front conning towers.

"Number One, full emergency speed on the engines.

Lift the limiting gates.

Engineer, full reverse power, NOW, on the arrester winches."

They both acted together.

His first officer removed the mechanical stops on his five sets of throttles, and pushed the diesel engines up to their limits as set by the electronic governors.

Above this the pistons would seize and damage the engine. They could operate in this mode only for five minutes. That would be more than enough time.

At the same time, the engineer was applying the maximum braking force to the aircraft as possible through the arrester wires.

Captain Petersen felt his tanker increase speed steadily, until sixty-five knots showed on his screen.

That was as much as he could get.

They saw the aircraft slewing from side to side, and eventually end up in a sideways skid with the port wing ahead of the starboard.

"She's going over the edge, Captain.

The computer predicts an overrun speed of ten knots.

Do you want crash barriers?"

"Thank you Number One. Lift them now."

The first barrier was the tennis court net stretched across the deck for the undercarriage to engage.

The second barrier was along the front lip of the tanker deck, and was a metal wall one metre in height, which could take the force of impact from an aircraft as heavy as the Vulcan with ease.

This was the thump that I had felt which shot me forward into the seat straps.

The momentum of the aircraft carried forward and compressed the front hydraulic spring in the nose wheel strut, onto which the weight of the aircraft crunched.

The port main wheel hit the barrier at the same time, and the back end of the Vulcan plus the starboard wing lifted up, and started to tip the port wing down towards the water.

"Engineer, maximum emergency power on the starboard reverse winches."

Whilst this was being done, Captain Peteresen looked at the wind direction on his screen. It was still twenty degrees to starboard.

He looked at the wings on the Vulcan, tipped up on the front of his tanker, and immediately thought of his sailing days with his father in their dinghy.

His brain was working out the relative speeds of his tanker, the direction and speed of the wind, and the angle of the wings to the resultant wind vector.

"Number One, alter course thirty degrees starboard."

"Aye, aye, Sir."

He felt the tanker shift around, and at the same time kept his eye on the pitot tube just breaking the white horses on the wave crests.

He was cool.

He was calm.

There was no need for dramatics.

They all knew what would happen if it tipped over. They would suffer just as quickly.

In fact they were all cool and calm.

It was to do with the fact that they were all in their second lives, because all three of them were survivors from the Persian Gulf attack four years previously.

Getting that Vulcan back onto the deck again was their contribution to the revenge they all felt.

"On heading Sir, and I've managed a bit more speed by adjusting the hydrofoils, but we're at maximum speed now.

I can't get any more"

They looked at the wing tip just breaking the tops of the waves.

They saw the outer ailerons lower slowly down to strike the waves... and saw the wing tip bounce across the surface.

It remained like that for a full minute.

"He's holding it Sir.

It hasn't dropped any further.

The winches are stopping it falling over, and the ailerons are stopping the wing tipping in.

All we need now is a sky hook, or heavy helicopter, to lift it further up."

"No possibility Number One. They're too far away."

He crossed his fingers and prayed.

* * *

Ray and I were very busy after the shock wore off.

It took about two seconds for both of us to realise what we had to do.

I pulled the stick fully to the right, to drop the ailerons on the port wing into the water, and to raise those on the starboard side into the airflow, to help push that wing downwards.

I pushed forward with my left foot to turn the rudder to the left. This would apply the airflow pressure on the vertical fin to the right, to push it back towards the deck.

I held the controls like that and looked at the port wing tip.

I could see and feel the bounce and knew instinctively that we had caught it in time.

"Ray, isolate the fuses in the lower reverse thrust hydraulic system, and return the plates to their normal position."

There was about two seconds delay before he found them in the computer database.

"Got them Peter. Give me thirty seconds to get them out."

He pulled open an electrical panel on the rear cabin bulkhead, and found the four fuses he was looking for.

"Pulling them out now Peter.

Check the engine power."

I eased back on the throttles carefully, and kept a beady eye on the wing tip.

I had no idea what the present thrust was doing, but if I changed the power too fast it could have tipped the wing.

Not having a PHD in advanced aerodynamics and a programmable hand held computer tends to limit one's decisions in moments of stress like this, so one just had to suck it and see!

The wing continued to bounce so I held the power at seventy per cent of its maximum.

"Ok Ray.

Fuses out now.

Starboard engine first."

I felt a kick forward, as the lower part of the reverse jet efflux shot rearwards, and felt the barrier net strain under the force.

There was another short kick as the port fuses came out, but no further movement from the aircraft.

It was well and truly jammed against the front crash barrier.

Ray came up to the front and looked out of the window.

He went yellow.

I looked at him.

"You're going to be sick aren't you?"

He nodded, as he looked at the boiling water surging underneath the front of the tanker, twenty feet below him.

"I never could stand boats. I always got sea sick."

And with that he buried his head in a sick bag.

I looked at him with sincere sympathy. I knew how he felt as I nearly went through it myself as we tipped over.

"Can I have your bacon sandwich when you've finished?" I asked.

He buried his head once more, and disappeared down the ladder.

Ray never could take a joke. He had no sense of humour.

I pushed the starboard throttles forward as gently as I could.

The reverse thrust plate was still in position on the top of the jet efflux, and soon the force built up to the point where I could see the wing tip lift up a fraction from the wave tops.

A bit more power and I saw a definite rise.

We were winning.

I pushed forward to full power, and the engine surged to maximum thrust.

At the same time I stabbed the afterburner button for one second.

It was just like bonfire night, and it worked.

The red jet of flame shot over one hundred feet into the air, and the resultant downwards force slammed the starboard undercarriage down onto the deck, so hard that the aircraft bounced back up again.

I pulled back on all the throttles, cut the afterburner, pulled on the parking brake, and gritted my teeth.

The winches did their work as well.

As the aircraft bounced up again, they pulled at full power against the undercarriage legs, and by the time we came to rest the aircraft had been pulled back ten metres, and was facing forward into the wind; with myself and the nose section directly above the bow of the tanker.

We looked like the flying wing mascot on the front bonnet of a Rolls Royce, as it sedately cruised down the motorway.

I had a breather for a couple of seconds.

It was Captain Petersen who spoke first.

"Zero One, This is the Pride of Free Enterprise.

Welcome aboard.

Well done."

I breathed a heavy sigh of relief. We had arrived at long last.

Ray came up front looking a bit better. He looked down at the water again.

"That was a bit close Peter.

You'll have to practice that a bit more. I don't think you got the flare out correct."

I was about to offer some derogatory remark, when the tanker came an again. It was a list of instructions to carry out for the refuelling.

"Zero One, parking brakes off please while we tow you back to the start point"

I acknowledged and left the team to attend to the roll back.

They had reduced speed in order that they could work on the deck without being blown off. A low vehicle coupled up to the nose wheel and guided us backwards, as the winches pulled the arrester cables aft.

The aircraft ended up on the second tanker from the rear of the ship.

As it passed the start point of tankers two and three, a flat hook was attached to a connection point between the nose wheel tyres, with a cable attached to it.

These were the steam catapult attachments for our take off.

The tug pushed us backwards to the refuelling point on the touchdown line.

"Watch you don't push us over pal," said Ray on the UHF.

"Don't worry mate. The rear barrier is up.

We're not going through all that again."

Captain Petersen came on the radio.

"Zero One, message from Gan.

Would you like a lift? We can take you there if you wish."

I was very tempted.

Ray shook his head.

"Thank you for your hospitality Captain, but we'll make tracks as soon as possible.

Please advise Gan control for us."

The refuelling crew filled us to about fifty per cent capacity. It was enough to get us to the island and light enough for us to get off from the tanker safely.

We'd had enough drama for the day. A nice quiet trip was all we asked for now.

It took only fifteen minutes for the ground crew to get us ready.

Ray replaced the fuses and all was now serviceable within the aircraft.

The fuel was in and the first catapult hook fitted to the nose wheel. I could see the three cables lying on the deck ahead of me.

One of the crew walked to a point so that I could see him. He pointed to the door and opened his hands like crocodile jaws opening up.

"Ray, open the door. I think we have a visitor."

I heard it open, and the ladder rattle as it was fitted into place. There were a few shouts of conversation above the engine noise, then the door shut again.

"What was that about?" I asked.

"Oh, nothing much, just a parcel for Gan."

"Zero One, final check. Are you both OK?"

Ray nodded.

"Yes, let's get going"

I acknowledged their message.

"Thank you Enterprise.

Ready for takeoff.

I'll call you 'power on' for the catapults"

"Thank you Captain, have a good trip."

Captain Petersen was always very polite on the radio and with his crew. It was a very reassuring calm voice and it boosted our flagging morale.

The tanker increased its speed, and I felt it rising on the wedge at the front of the ship.

The flat top rippled and hinged, as the five sections took it in turn to ride up on the hydrofoils.

When this occurred the airspeed on the screen in front of me increased rapidly to seventy-five knots. We just needed another eighty to get airborne.

The tanker had already reduced our take off speed by half.

The rest would be easy.

"Ok Ray?"

"Yes, all systems are serviceable. Ready for takeoff."

I pushed the throttles forward to half power, and waited for the catapult cables to take the strain.

I watched them straighten up and vibrate with tension as they prepared for the rapid pull.

I held the brakes hard on and pushed the throttles up to three quarters power. We were now as ready as we would ever be.

"Ok Ray, call the control room now."

I switched the afterburners on, checked the power then pushed the throttles forward.

At the same time the catapults operated and I was slammed hard against the seat.

The deck was a blur of steel, and then there was the open sea and the blue of the sky.

We ended up airborne before we realised it.

Ray gasped.

"Strewth. Can I go back and get my stomach?"

"No don't bother.

Just open that bottle of rum the crew gave us whilst we still have one."

He unwrapped the parcel.

Printed on the label was a message:

BEST NAVAL MEDICINE. DRINK OFTEN BETWEEN MEALS

It was just what the Captain ordered! I pressed the UHF transmit button.

"Enterprise, thank you very much for all your help down there.

Much appreciated."

There was a pause. Captain Petersen came on the radio.

"Thank you Zero One. A very entertaining afternoon.

It wouldn't have done you any good if you had fallen in, we couldn't have got you out.

None of us can swim"

I looked at Ray and just shook my head.

So it was true after all.

Sailors can't swim!

"Captain Petersen, You're joking. I don't believe it.

Even my old Mum has got her beginner's certificate, for struggling with fortitude and dexterity against all odds across two widths of the swimming baths, and you lot can't even do that.

I don't know what this organisation's getting to, employing useless fish heads that can't swim."

There was a slight pause.

"Neither do I, Captain Barten, and it's getting worse.

Fish heads that can't swim, and now ex-brylcreem boys that can't fly or even land their aeroplanes.

You just can't get good staff these days. I suppose we have to make the best of what we have.

Have a good trip, gentlemen.

My regards to all at Gan."

Ray smiled and pressed the UHF transmit button.

"And to you, Sir."

I looked down and saw his Enterprise flagship below skimming the waves, riding high on the foils.

If ever a man deserved success, it was Olaf Petersen.

"We'll just say goodbye to them Ray. Keep your eyes an them while I turn around."

I turned the aircraft to the left, in a wide circle until I was directly behind them again, pointing towards the flat deck.

I then selected the airbrakes out, and reduced power for a normal landing.

When we were about two miles away, Ray selected the undercarriage down.

The high-speed runway was now directly ahead of us, gliding across the ocean smoothly on its foils.

They saw us on the cameras flying over the sea towards them. About a mile from them I rocked my wings twice before transmitting.

"Enterprise, Zero One, finals, three greens, landing instructions please."

Back came the reply.

"Zero One, you are clear to roll.

The runway is clear"

I eased back on the throttles gently and flew the Vulcan carefully down towards the deck. As we got closer I selected the airbrakes to the high drag position and saw the deck of the first tanker slide gracefully underneath the nose of the aircraft.

The aircraft touched down softly onto the deck of the second tanker, the tyres rumbling over the steel surface.

Ray selected the airbrakes in and, I pushed the throttles fully forward.

The aircraft rolled onto the third and fourth tanker decks, and got airborne halfway down the fifth.

Ray selected the undercarriage up, and we flew straight ahead until the wheels were up into the fuselage and wings.

"Enterprise, Zero One climbing away.

Please advise Gan Control."

I pulled the joystick slowly backwards until we were vertical, then switched on the afterburners.

We went up like a rocket, the flames stretching almost four hundred feet behind us as we climbed to height.

It was the first time that we had let the aircraft have its 'head' and it was powerful.

We decided to stop it at sixty thousand feet; otherwise we would have gone sub-orbital and never have reached Gan.

It was still vertical... and climbing!

We saw the tanker below us on its way north, and I thought of Olaf Petersen and his crew down there as I flew along. They had saved us from going over the front of their ship, and suddenly I felt very humble.

We had been lucky.

Very lucky indeed.

I hoped that one day, quite soon, we could return the favour. They needed the sort of luck that we had if they were to survive the Gulf runs.

I also hoped the favour could be returned before that luck ran out!

Ray came up later with two glasses.

"I think we both deserve a drink, Peter. That was too close for comfort.

You did well to get us out of that one mate.

Your very good health."

He was right.

It was the closest brush with St Peter that either of us had. Mind you, he would most likely have been extremely disappointed.

With our track records, I reckon that the devil himself had reserved our shovels, as it was more likely that we were destined to stoke the boilers than pluck harp strings.

"Thanks Ray.

Bottoms up."

It was another two hours to go, so I let the autopilot do the work, and just watched the flight instruments as I sipped my grog.

The Royal Navy may have scrubbed the rum ration...

But we hadn't.

Chapter 10. Gan

It was a leisurely trip from the refuelling point to Gan.

It only took about two hours and I regret to say that my top eyelids met my bottom eyelids in the middle of my eyes. I came back to the world when I felt a finger dig into the side of my shoulder.

"Are we awake then?"

"What do you mean? I've been watching the instruments all the time and listening to everything that's going on," I replied.

"Oh, that's all right then. So you didn't mind when I switched on your microphone and transmitted your snores to Gan control. You can hear the recording of what you said to them when we land."

"You'd sell your own grandmother if you had the chance."

Ray grinned and painted to the port VDU.

"The message is to land as soon as possible."

He pressed a button and changed the screen to the radar picture.

"And there it is, directly on the nose about fifteen minutes away. Just follow the radar indications.

We don't want you to work too hard. Let the autopilot do it all. It seems to be the only thing around here that knows what it's doing.

At least, it's the only pilot that seems to be working."

"Go and play with your switches," I suggested.

It had been almost fifteen years since I had last seen Gan. Not that there's much to see.

Once you've said the name, that's it. The question you have to ask yourself when you first see it is:

"Is the runway on the island or is the island under the runway?", because that's all it is.

A runway on an island, which is the length of the runway. If you walk off either end of the concrete you get your feet wet.

If you do the same thing when your feet are in an aeroplane, then you'd better get your umbrella up pretty sharpish, because the Gan guano's going to hit the fan!

It used to be a refuelling post for RAF aircraft flying to the Far East in the 'olden days' but it has been disused for years now.

The only occupants tend to be the indigenous little frogs, which are about half an inch long, coloured green, and sit on the green surface of the island contemplating what they're going to do for the rest of the day - until you squelch all over them, which you could very easily do, especially if you're colour blind!

The size of the blip on the screen was concerning me though.

It was too big for the island I remember.

I fed the TV signal to the port VDU and selected long range.

"Ray, have a look. What do you make of this?"

He selected the TV picture on the rear screen.

"It's too far to see clearly but it could be a fleet of ships."

The closer we got the more distinct the picture became. It was indeed a fleet of ships, but the largest concentration of vessels that I had ever seen.

When we got to about ten miles from the island we could pick out at least a dozen oil tankers, most of them ULCCs.

"I reckon it's a bunkering facility for ships crossing the Indian Ocean." Ray volunteered.

"I've counted over a hundred so far on the radar, and that's only on half the screen. A proper little Paddy's market by the look of it."

I was looking into the bay now and could see what he meant.

Granted I could not see very far in the twilight, but the ships stretched for at least five miles north of the island. Maybe it was the gathering darkness, or maybe my eyes were tired after the long flight, but they all looked different.

The closer we got the clearer it all became.

"Ray," I said sombrely,

"Have a look out of your window while it's still light."

There were six or seven large tankers beached right next to the runway, the superstructures all rusted away, the oil tanks burnt and twisted; and the end two ships were on their sides, with the bridges ripped apart.

I saw at least four British cruisers burnt out with gaping holes in their sides.

It is extremely difficult to tell the difference between American, French, Russian and British merchant vessels when they have been blown to bits by bombs, so I didn't try to establish the various nationalities.

I didn't even try to count them, and neither did Ray. We just flew round and round the bay and looked at the carnage.

It was a graveyard for dead ships... and I don't mean 'dead ships', which are ships without their crews in the middle of the night, I mean ships that have had their guts torn right out of them, and the bulkheads split apart.

"Peter, on your right about a mile."

Ray sounded serious. I peered through the gloom and hoped it wasn't what we thought.

We had to go and look to find out for ourselves.

The instruction to "Land as soon as possible" could wait for a while. I flew slowly around the bay to get a better view... and our worst fears were justified.

"They kept quiet about that." I said to Ray.

It was the Queen Mary 2.

She was on her side, split in half, the stern gaping wide open and as black as burnt pitch.

I could clearly see at least four torpedo holes in the inverted hull. The bow had separated from the stern and the keel split completely down the middle.

She had been carrying United Nations troops the last time I heard about her, and I dread to think how many were on board when she got hit.

Ray spoke.

"I think I've found the Charles de Gaulle on the western edge of the bay."

He was right.

The flight deck pitched downwards with the huge bronze propellers clear of the water. It looked as if four bombs had gone through the flat top, but one would have been enough, with a carrier full of aircraft and fuel.

All around it, scattered like debris, were small ships, landing craft, lifeboats...

The radio burst into life.

"Zero One, when you're ready, perhaps you'd like to join us on the island?"

I looked at Ray. He nodded, "I've seen enough, let's get down."

I returned the controller's call.

"Control, Zero One, we'll land in five minutes."

They were good down there. They knew exactly what they were doing with that landing message.

It made sure that we saw what they wanted us to see before we landed.

I had intended staying at height until darkness fell before descending.

I decided to use the TV head-up unit and let the aircraft do an automatic landing on its own. I set the two crosses on each side of the runway at the touchdown point.

There is no margin for error at Gan. It's either on the concrete, or in the sea, and I was making sure it was the concrete.

Besides, I hadn't got an umbrella!

Ray set up the programme, the aircraft followed the instructions from the runway microwave landing system and it glided down like the Shuttle landing at Edwards Air Force base in California.

All I had to do was apply the landing brakes, and stop it on the runway.

It was getting dark now, so I followed the yellow marshalling truck off the runway, and along the perimeter track towards the old hangars; but it turned in the other direction, towards the sea.

Something was wrong, and I stopped the aircraft, just in case the driver had made a mistake.

"Zero One, do as you're told and follow the truck, there's a good chap."

He had seen me stop.

I thought, "Well, he's the boss," so I did as I was told, and turned down towards the flashing blue light.

We went half way down the peritrack, then turned out towards the beach; and went across a wide ramp over the sand...

It was very cleverly done.

They had cut out the complete side of one of the rusting tankers that were beached on the island, and it dropped down like a drawbridge to link with the peritrack.

The other tankers had received the same treatment, and they had been welded together. From the outside they looked derelict, but inside was a large hangar space, big enough to hold three Vulcans.

"Zero One, welcome to Gan, please chop your engines."

We did, they raised the drawbridge, and the island was 'disused' again.

It was good to be out into fresh air and to walk around. We must have been cooped up for about twelve hours or so.

The computer could tell us to the ten thousandth of a second, but it doesn't need to stretch and shower like human beings have to do.

An engineer approached us.

"Mr Barten, Mr Preston, could you come with me please?"

He led us to the control room, and that's where we saw our colleague who had controlled us at the Waddington bunker.

I knew the situation was grave as soon as I saw his face.

"I'm afraid that there has been a major disaster at Fulbeck. I think you had better read this."

It was all in the signal.

We were devastated.

"There is another signal. We received it four hours ago."

The message was quite clear for everyone to understand.

:OPERATION TO PROCEED IMMEDIATELY:

"You'll take off tomorrow evening just before twilight.

Everything will be ready then. We'll call you at midday."

There was no need for him to say any more.

We'd had enough.

Tomorrow was another day.

I looked at Ray. He knew what I was thinking.

"We are doing the right thing, aren't we?"

He looked at the signals, then looked up at me.

"I don't know, Peter, we'll never know, but I sincerely hope that we are. I really do."

"So do I, Ray, so do I."

* * *

I thought of all those unfortunate people who once lived at Fulbeck, and wondered at the price we sometimes had to pay.

"Is it worth it?" I asked myself,

"Is it all worth it?"

And I still haven't found anyone who can tell me.

Nobody at all.

Chapter 11. Preparations

I did not need their midday call.

The sleep that I had managed to get on the flight here must have been deep, because I felt quite awake now. I lay in the bunk for a few minutes, then got myself up and about.

Ray was still flat out so I left him. I found the galley, helped myself, then strolled around the tankers.

It was quite a professional job. Last night I only saw the hangar and control room but there was more than that.

The ships had been restored on the inside, and gave the appearance of being fully operational, with all the services being used.

It was only the external features that gave the impression of dereliction. As a cover it was as good as one could imagine.

The tanker nearest the island was the one which had been used for the control room. The bridge to the rear of the vessel overlooked the island, and acted as lookout, walkway, ship and aircraft control area, and communications.

I could see all over the island, a flat patch of green separated by the runway.

On the other side, where the old airport complex used to be, was a Tristar.

I hadn't heard it come in, so I must have been asleep on its arrival.

There was a pair of binoculars in the locker, so I used them. It was all silver, no markings, number or any means of identification. Rather like our Vulcan.

I presumed that it had the same painting job done on it. I could not see any activity around it at all.

There were some vehicles down by the jetty in the inner lagoon, but not a sole in sight.

"If you look to your left you might find something interesting."

Now, there are some voices that grate on your teeth.

Others have that refined cultural touch that is in bred in certain people.

There are some that are plummy, and silver spooned, where individuals try to appear better than their station in life; but this was none of these.

It was supercilious, sickly, and spoke down to you as if you were a piece of over ripe pig manure.

It was a good job I had left the galley, otherwise the milk would have turned sour.

"What do you want, Le Boustarde?"

"Just come to look after your interests, old boy.

Making sure that you and your friend don't stroll too far."

I felt like heaving over the side of the tanker, to give the fish my breakfast.

Even for a military policeman that statement showed a certain lack of brain cell. Where the hell did he think we could go stuck in the middle of the Indian Ocean, with about three thousand miles of sea in either direction?

My God, he was thick.

I was about to tell him so him so in no uncertain terms...

And then I noticed that he was surrounded by my two new drinking partners, Mammoth and Goliath. They stood either side of him. It looked like a little shrimp between two whales.

I could feel my fingers tightening around the body of the binoculars.

"Don't throttle the glasses, old boy; you might need some when you grow older.

That's if you ever manage to grow up."

I had my right arm up in the classic baseball pitcher's position, ready to throw them at him, when I realised that he wasn't worth the expense.

He knew he had won again, merely by the fact that I had lost my temper.

Each of them had that 'come and have a go if you dare, make my day' type of grin.

We stayed like that until they casually took their time, and left the way they came in. I was still shaking with frustrated temper when our controller arrived.

"I take it Le Boustarde's been here.

Say no more. He does that to everyone.

I don't know where they got him from, but I hope they don't go back for anymore."

I had found a fellow human being at last.

"I'm just seeing the hospital ship in, you can stay if you want."

It was being towed by two deep sea tugs, through the gap into the bay.

Down the right hand side two barges were lashed up tight, to reduce the heavy list.

The white paint with the big red cross on the side looked as if it had been raked with shell fire, there were blackened holes from bow to stern.

Part of the bridge was gone completely, and I could see the officers through the open side.

"We'll patch her up with plates from the old wrecks and she'll be back out again this evening with a new crew," he told me.

I realised now what the Tristar had arrived for.

It was an airborne casualty evacuation for somebody, but who?

"And the Tristar?" I asked.

"That's for our chaps. We fly them to Socotra island. It's nice and discrete.

We have our main hospital there, and we do our best before we send them back again. A lot of them never make it.

The French use their own facilities in Ethiopia, the Russians fly theirs back to Afghanistan, and the Yanks to their base down south."

I watched it as it limped in and dropped anchor. The small boats took off the dead and wounded, and a regular shuttle of activity occurred between various points immediately around it.

I looked again at the war damage to it.

"When did it catch that lot?"

It was a heavy sigh.

"We couldn't get it out from Bahrain quickly enough, and it got hit by both sides.

It lost its escorts on the way in, and had none on its return until half way to the Strait."

He looked hard at me.

"She's the lucky one. We lost the other.

Her sister ship caught three torpedoes and it went down in five minutes."

He turned and looked at the hospital ship.

"That's when she got her packet.

She was turning back to see if there were any survivors, when the other sub hit her. We got there just in time to stop her sinking."

My knees weakened and I could feel nausea creeping upwards.

When it reached my throat,I'm afraid to say that it had a greater effect than even Le Boustarde.

Human nature must have degenerated to an all time low when hospital ships were prime targets.

"Can you please tell me exactly what's going on here?"

He put the binoculars down and saw the uncertainty on my face.

"OK, let's go to the galley. We'll find a coffee pot and a map, then I'll show you."

Ray joined us and heard the details as well.

The whole of the Persian Gulf was an active war zone, not just between the two main belligerents, but it included a United Nations force composed of some of the members of the Security Council.

The remainder had either left because they could not afford the colossal expense of the war, or had been blown out of it a long time ago.

I asked my main question.

"Why the hell doesn't anybody do something about this, on a political basis, to stop it?"

He drew hard on his cigarette.

"You are now in the Civilian Sector of the United Nations force, and as such have no political affiliations at all.

That applies to all of us; otherwise we would not be here. We receive our support from the United Nations, and operate quietly and discretely.

There are officially no military operations from the United Nations at all within the Gulf, but if we weren't there then the whole of the conflict would spread outwards, into the Indian Ocean and beyond.

If that happens, then the politicians and the major governments would have to make some very unpopular decisions back home; and what is more important to them, their individual economies would suffer because of that black stuff that's pouring out of ground straight into their pockets.

Once that gets affected then the tears will begin, bankers will start to weep, and the all the stuff that our pin striped gentleman told you at Cockfosters will suddenly start to come true.

By doing it this way, certain powerful people can keep their noses clean, and look good on television.

It might begin to dawn on you that it's to their individual advantage to keep it all going, which is exactly what's happening.

Nobody is going to make the decision to stop it all, and ruin the gravy train.

If, by any unfortunate chance to them, the proverbial does hit the fan, they make damn sure that they have got a fireproof umbrella, and it's some poor lower minion who catches it."

Ray spoke then,

"And in the meantime, of course, money still circulates, certain industries and people benefit.

Everybody's got jobs, because they are either here, or producing all this hardware, and up front everything is rosy in the garden."

"Yes," said our man,

"As long as it's retained in the Persian Gulf, where the unfortunate consumers are creating the industrial demand.

The official United Nations force only acts as a policeman outside the area."

"How long has this being going on for?" I asked him.

"Well, I've been here three years, and I can only assume it's been well before that."

We continued talking at length after that, as he was very interesting to talk to.

We had only seen him before in the light as one of our controllers, but now we saw him as the man he really was. It was most revealing. You could actually see the mask lifting away.

* * *

The aircraft needed a full check, in which we all participated.

They had turned it around with one of the big tugs, and it was now facing towards the drawbridge, ready for us this evening.

I did my bit with the switches in the cockpit, climbed down the ladder reading some figures, and sat down on some thirty five gallon oil drums, on the hangar floor underneath the port wing.

I took out my calculator and made sure the fuel contents were sufficient for tonight's trip.

I had nothing else to do, so I watched the ground crew for half an hour or so getting on with their various jobs.

It was time for one of our little 'chats', so I got down, rubbed the circulation back again and looked at the drums.

I read the markings on the top of each one.

Four of them had big white stencils on them:

: AVIATION FUEL. NO SMOKING WITHIN FIFTY YARDS:

And the fifth was marked:

: DANGER. 188 OCTANE AIRCRAFT GASOLINE:

I was fuming.

Talk about fire risk.

The idiot that did this could have blown the whole thing up. I stormed into the control office and played merry hell.

"Calm down." our man said

"They came off the Tristar this morning.

Those oil drums, as you call them, happen to be the bombs you're dropping tonight."

I nearly fainted on the spot.

"You mean to say that those drums, casually parked under that wing, are five atomic weapons?"

He was working at the time.

He stopped suddenly, and stared up at me, a worried look on his face.

"You didn't go anywhere near them did you?"

I was furious.

"I course I did. How was I to know what they were?

What stupid moron put them there in the first place without any signs up?

I've been sitting on them for the last half hour."

He covered his face with his hands.

"You're not married are you?"

"No, not yet."

He looked relieved.

"In that case it doesn't matter too much. I thought it was going to be serious."

I looked back towards the aircraft.

Two engineers in blue overalls had tipped one of the bombs over onto its side, and were rolling it across the hangar floor towards the bomb bay.

I just pointed; speechless, eyes wide open.

Ray came into the room and looked.

"What's up, Peter, you look as if you've seen a ghost?"

I just pointed, stabbing my finger towards the two men, who were trying to lift the heavy drum onto a trolley.

Our controller by this time was slowly edging sideways, his back to the wall, towards the rear exit of the control room.

Ray turned and saw the two technicians staggering under weight of the drum. It must have weighed a ton by the look them.

"What's your problem? Those are only the empty outer cases.

Didn't they tell you?

They're going to put the nuclear cores in afterwards when they're all loaded in the bomb bay."

I was around and across that room in a flash, but I was too late.

The controller was out of that door, and down the corridor, running as if the hounds of hell were after him.

"I'll get you," I shouted after him.

"Next time I see you, I'll throttle the living daylights out of you."

One up to him I suppose.

He really had me going then.

I made myself a coffee and sat down. Ray was sitting opposite me reading a map... smiling to himself.

"Fancy a trip out tonight, Peter?"

I looked up.

"What do you mean by that?"

"I just thought you'd like to go across the airfield to the Doc's, to see if there's any damage!"

The coffee cup disintegrated against the wall, behind the recently vacated space that he had occupied half a second before.

"And you can clear off as well," I shouted after his retreating heels.

We were busy after that.

We met the nuclear man after he had inserted the atomic cores into the outer casing drums.

The procedures that we had to follow were those practiced over and over again in the aircraft.

Each bomb was controlled by the rear computer, which Ray operated, and the flight computer which I controlled.

If any of the parameters were out of limits then they would not function, and we would have to start again.

The science people had taken into account the depth of the Strait at each point where we were to drop the weapons, and had adjusted the strengths of the cores accordingly.

We could not just drop the drums anywhere; we had to put each one in its correct place commencing with number one.

If we missed out on any of the drops, then we would have to go back to the starting point and try again.

If we couldn't drop any of them then we had to return to Gan.

Just to get the first four drops accurate had taken us hours of practice in our simulator aircraft, and that was sitting still in a hangar!

The whole operation depended on the fifth weapon.

That had to be dropped last of all, because it had a transmitter within it to trigger the other four, otherwise there would be no simultaneous explosion; and that was the main objective of the whole operation.

When that number five went off it would be the biggest bang this side of Timbuktu, and I didn't want to be around when that happened.

We had our procedures to follow after dropping them all, which would allow us to return to Gan later on.

It is no secret to say how we were to drop them.

It is common sense.

Because the bombs were barrel shaped, they each had the aerodynamic properties of a brick, so they would need stabilising as they fell through the air towards the ground; otherwise they would tumble all over the place.

We were going to spin them fast in the bomb bay, to turn them into large heavy gyroscopes, and then drop them.

The rotation would provide the necessary stability as they dropped through the airflow, gravity would play its part, down they would go, and drop into the water.

At least that's the theory.

All we had to do was get to the right place, at the right time, at the right speed, at the right height, at the right attitude, at the right... etc, etc, etc.

That was the practical.

It all had to work, and come together exactly when we wanted it to, otherwise the whole thing would be a washout, and a complete waste of everyone's time.

The whole of the afternoon was spent in preparation, as it was likely to be a long night.

The aircraft men prepared the aeroplane, the control men prepared their plans, the nuclear men prepared the bombs... and we prepared ourselves.

At our departure meal in the galley, we had a few more visitors than we had when we arrived.

The room was full of faces watching us.

I felt like the main contender for the last supper.

One of the engineers came across, looking very solemn, holding his beret in both his hands. He looked embarrassed.

"Mr Barten, Mr Preston. The chaps have sent me across to ask you a question."

"What is it Bill?" I asked.

He twisted his beret as he spoke.

"Well, you see, it's a bit like this.

The rations are pretty grim round here, and we were all wondering..."

He looked behind him at this point.

All the others waved encouragement at him, and told him to get on with it.

He turned and looked down at us.

"We were just wondering...

It could be a bit dangerous for you both on the operation tonight...

If you don't come back, could we have your eggs?"

I looked at Ray.

He nearly choked on his fillet steak and button mushrooms.

I then saw the rest of the engineers.

They were all curled up against the wall, laughing and waving their beers in our direction.

The 'messenger' skipped it back to them as fast as his little legs could carry him.

They all got three 'clear offs'; two stronger expressions, and four airmen's farewells from each of us before they disappeared and left us alone.

They were a good bunch of fellows. They'd looked after us well since our arrival.

They'd appreciate the case of beer that we'd arranged for them after we had taken off.

That's if they hadn't already found it!

* * *

The departure from Gan was a bit more dignified and refined than our previous, from another place.

They pulled us across the drawbridge onto the peritrack, and even to the extent of lining us up on the runway.

All we did, in the literary sense, was switch on and go.

It took half a minute for the engines to wind up, two minutes for the computers to check everything was serviceable, and a further twenty seconds to get airborne.

"Zero One, this is Gan Control.

Best of luck. Have a good trip."

We were on our way.

* * *

Le Boustarde watched them climb away and disappear into the clouds.

He could see the red exhaust gases from the jets, climbing up into the black sky as the aircraft gained altitude.

He drew the last drag on his cigarette, then held the butt between the thumb and second finger of his right hand for a few minutes as he watched, then flicked it high into the air.

The glowing tip curved upwards for a while then fell slowly down, down, down until it hit the water and fizzled out.

He looked at the ripples on the water caused by the small projectile, and watched them get smaller and smaller... until, eventually, they disappeared altogether.

He lifted his eyes, and gazed hard into the distant horizon to the north of the island, looking for the aircraft.

It was nowhere to be seen.

Chapter 12. Running In

We did all our safety and flight checks on the transit to our first reference point.

I wanted to be sure that when we entered the declared zone we stood, if not a hundred percent chance of success, then something damn close to it.

We checked each computer individually, then ran a test programme in order that they could check each other. The parameters that we had to stick to were very tight, and if those electronic brains didn't work we may as well have packed up and gone home.

Our Gan gentlemen had not let us down.

We could forget the small discrepancies that the computers picked up. They were not going to effect the final outcome. Ray just programmed them out, and we ignored them.

The plan was to fly up to the Gulf of Oman, descend fast to get as low as we possibly dared, go straight in, drop the five bombs, then get out fast for the tanker rendezvous.

I stopped thinking about the things that could go wrong.

It does no good to dwell on these matters, you just have to deal with them as they arise.

"Everything looks all right, Peter.

When we get lower down select the TV camera for maximum range, and make sure we don't go too near any ships."

There would be a lot of tankers offshore on the Muscat side of the Omani Gulf, so the plan was to fly further north, closer to the Iranian coast; then once we had passed the port of Jask, curve around to the right, to be about ten miles off the coast opposite Ras Ab Kuh.

With a bit of luck, if we could pick up the lighted flares at the oil refinery at Bandar Abbas with the infra red camera, we could run straight in and let the computers do the rest... that's why they were so important.

We used the island of Masira as the point where we would start to descend.

The controllers at Gan knew where we were all the time.

The main computer was linked to the communication room back at the tanker through the Skynet satellite, so they probably knew a lot more than we did.

What was of greater importance to us, was the fact that they could feed in additional information directly into our flight control computer.

That would give me an update on what the aircraft needed to do at any given time.

It was through this link that the signal would be routed from the fifth weapon, to ensure a simultaneous explosion from all five.

It couldn't be done otherwise, as we would be miles away at the time.

"Masira to the left, Peter."

I switched on the television and picked out the port of Gwadar on the Pakistani coastline. That was my second reference point.

No ships were in the way. Everything was satisfactory in the aeroplane, so down we went.

It was a good job we had the TV, because it was as black as the ace of spades down there. Not a light in sight.

The flight computer did the main work, I just made sure that it did it correctly.

It took the aircraft down to about two thousand feet above the sea, at the selected speed, then it just followed the visual markers which I had put on the TV screen for Gwadar.

* * *

Nothing to it this flying; especially this trip, 'they' had told us.

Just sit back and watch the passing scenery.

I noted however that the great 'They' were sitting on their backsides in a nice warm comfortable lounge, watching our progress on their monitors.

I also noted that none of the great 'They' had actually volunteered to join us, to watch the so called passing scenery!

* * *

"I can see Jask now Peter, but you have to go further out as you turn around the coast.

There's a fleet of ships in the way."

"Ok, feed it onto the port screen. I've got Gwadar on the other one."

By interfacing both screens and letting the TV equipment follow the port screen I could find out what the ships were.

"It's a tanker convoy coming out of Muscat. We'll pass to the north of it," I advised Ray.

I set one visual marker to a point to the north of the line of tankers, and the other ten miles out from the port of Jask.

I pressed a button and the aircraft did all the rest.

We went nowhere near them.

From Jask to Bandar Abbas it's about one hundred and fifty miles, and we were going to start dropping the bombs fifty miles out from the Bandar Abbas breakwater every ten miles as we approached the city.

The refinery was one mile from the harbour entrance, and that's what the TV was hoping to pick up as we turned around the coast.

Once again it was Ray who found it first.

It wasn't surprising, considering he had help from the very brave 'They'.

Our heroes, sitting in the safety of their tanker about two and a half thousand miles away.

I bet they're quaking in their boots, at the thought of us doing all the work!

"On the port screen now."

I did another interface, and looked very carefully at the screen.

We were coming up to the crucial point.

I wanted a relatively clear run for the first four drops, but the last one had to be clear of any ship in the area.

Large or small.

"Ray, have a look at the monitor.

Check the small boat that's at the seven mile point.

Feed it into the computer and tell me if it's in the way."

Yes, it was, he told me.

Our first big hitch, and it wasn't of our doing.

"Which direction is it travelling, and at what speed?"

He found out with help from our heroes back at Gan, and we decided to move closer to the Iranian coast before running in.

Five miles out should do it they reckoned, not ten.

"Feed that into your computer, Ray.

I'll set it on mine, and we'll let them cross check each other with Gan."

The computers did a full sequencing with each other whilst we flew in a circle. That little boat was causing us a lot of trouble.

It took about five minutes to re calculate all the dropping points.

Ray came onto the intercom when he had checked the figures.

"We start the run in from eighty five miles; the first drop is forty five and every ten miles from there.

The heights are on the altitude screen, and your speeds will show up on your head up display."

I could see them on the screen.

"Ok, you can start spinning the drums, and tell me when they're ready."

We had to do another full turn to the left before they got up to speed.

"Ok Peter, all five spinning."

We were turning in a wide circle to the left, about a hundred and fifty miles out from the refinery.

The weapons were now gyroscopes and ready for dropping; the television camera could pick up the flare, the little boat that caused all the bother was now out of the way, and all the computers were working.

"Feed page two onto the port screen, Ray."

This was the computer communication link from our controller.

He would know that everything was all right, and all we had to do now was wait for him to tell us what to do.

We went round and round for a good ten minutes, before the screen turned green.

If it turned red at any time from now on we would go back to Gan.

The camera was picking up the flare very strongly, and the flight computer steered the aircraft towards it.

At one hundred miles from the refinery it was right in front of us.

Ray had everything ready.

He would press two keys on the computer whenever we got to the dropping mileages.

One would make sure the bomb released from the aircraft.

The second to prepare the next bomb for dropping, and to tell the Gan computer what we were doing.

They would then know exactly when the fifth weapon dropped, so that they could switch on their timing programme to make sure they all went off together.

The first two bombs were no problem. Each of them spun down slowly and splashed into the Strait.

Unfortunately the third one was a mile closer than we wanted, and we had to recalculate the distances for the fourth and fifth bombs, to make sure that everything worked properly.

It was all to do with the shock waves after they exploded:

If they were too far apart then the waves would not interact through the water, to produce the desired effect.

The number four would now have to drop at fifteen miles, and the number five at six miles from the breakwater.

We restarted the run in from the twenty five mile point, towards the refinery flare, and followed the computers instructions.

Ray pressed the button and number four went exactly as planned.

Once the fifth one dropped we were going to depart rather rapidly; as the saying goes, with our stainless steel hot shovel.

"Peter, check that your final dropping speeds and heights are correct will you.

You're about five percent out."

I looked at the flight computer screen; re adjusted the throttles slightly, and altered the speed and height of the aircraft.

All we had to do now was wait:

At seven miles, Ray's finger pressed the first key, which told Gan we were ready to drop the last bomb, whilst I made sure that everything was perfect with the aircraft.

At six and a half miles I told Ray that everything looked good,

At six miles, exactly where we wanted to be, at the correct speed and height,

He pressed the second key, to release the bomb...

Chapter 13. Bouncing Bomb

Andrew Allen, our controller, was in the tanker control tower for our departure, and he watched us climb away and disappear.

He was in telephone contact with the radar computer operator, who could see the whole of the Indian Ocean area as far north as Muscat, by the Big Bird satellite transmitters in geostationary orbit above them.

"They are well to the north now, Andy, everything going well."

"Thank you, I'll come down in five minutes."

He saw the hospital ship sailing through the lagoon on her way back to the Gulf.

He picked up the microphone from the table.

"Bon voyage, Medic Two, best of luck."

"Thank you control," came the reply.

"Socotra One, ready for takeoff."

He looked across the island and saw the Tristar lined up on the runway.

"Clear take off, Socotra One, my regards to all on board. See you tomorrow."

"Thank you control."

He watched it climb out to the north west, before he went below and took his position in the control room.

"Where are they now?" He asked.

They looked at the computer monitor.

"Just east of Masira."

They monitored the aircraft as it flew north, descended towards Gwadar, re routed itself around the Muscat fleet and flew up to Jask.

"Andy, they've got a problem with a small boat in the dropping area."

Three of them looked at the screen, then fed the necessary information into the computer for a suitable answer.

They couldn't work it out without it. The problem was too complex.

"That seems quite reasonable.

Tell them to move five miles to the east for their run in, and use the alternative figures for the dropping distances."

The data was sent off to the aircraft main computer which Ray was using.

They could see the aircraft commence a left hand orbit, and watched the data from the bombs displayed on one of the monitors.

"They're holding off now at about one hundred miles, everything is serviceable, and they just need the final message to continue."

Andy picked up the telephone beside the monitor and pressed a green button.

He waited for about ten seconds for the line to connect.

"Everything satisfactory," was all he said, then waited.

It took about ten minutes before he replaced the receiver.

"Send the green code."

The controller pressed a button on his keyboard, and the signal went to the aircraft to colour the flight computer screen green.

He could change it to red within one second if necessary by pressing a different button.

"They're running in now, one hundred miles to the target."

The signals that Ray sent were recorded on the computer's memory disc, and could be analysed later.

"Number three is off station by one mile."

"No action required." Andy said.

The airborne computer could handle that one.

They saw the aircraft turn back to the twenty five mile point and recommence the run in.

The 'bomb gone' signal flashed beside the screen.

"Number four has dropped on its new station."

The controller looked at Andy.

"It looks all right for number five. I'm starting the timing sequence now."

He pressed the appropriate computer keys, which would synchronise the weapons.

"Everything is working satisfactory."

Andy looked at the screen as the aircraft approached the six mile point.

The controller's screen had a little light which would indicate when the bomb released from the aircraft.

They all watched as the Vulcan ran up towards the bomb release point, and saw the timer countdown marks ready on the screen to detonate the five weapons simultaneously.

At the appropriate moment, when Ray pressed the key on the main computer keyboard, the counters for the timer activated and the light flashed on.

It remained on for about half a second then went out... and stayed out...

It did not come an again.

* * *

The computers were now recording everything that happened in the finest detail.

When the information was replayed back at a speed which could be followed, the full picture could be seen - and this is what they did immediately afterwards.

Before the bomb left the aircraft I had to take the aircraft lower and faster.

As it dropped from the bomb bay the spin stabilised the drum in the airflow, and after one second it was down to fifty feet above the water.

It hit the surface very hard, tearing out a deep trough in the water approximately ten feet deep and twenty feet wide.

It stayed there for a moment, still spinning, then bounced upwards again.

The first four bombs had a backward spin, to make sure that they would travel vertically downwards through the water.

We wanted the fifth one to go horizontally forwards, so we put on a forward spin of approximately six hundred and seventy five revolutions per minute.

This first water strike was at the six mile point.

It bounced upwards and forwards, then hit the water again at a range of about three and three quarter miles.

By now twenty five percent of the forward momentum had gone, but the spin only reduced by ten percent.

The trough at this point was not as deep, but the resistance of the water was still sufficient to push the bomb up and forwards for the next bounce.

This occurred at about two miles from the shoreline.

It soared up again, retaining quite a large percentage of the spin, and reached a height of about eighty five feet.

For some reason it started to wobble at this point, and it hit the water again three quarters of a mile in front the break-water, over which it had to bounce in order to reach its final target.

The wobble had caused a small deflection to the right, but not sufficient to cause any serious problems.

It bounced over the harbour breakwater hitting the wooden customs shed, disintegrating it completely.

The first bounce on dry land was on the asphalt road between the two bonded warehouses.

It ripped off the top six inches of road surface, flew over the container park and complex of railway sidings, and landed half a mile further on, heading towards the Bandar Abbas main petroleum refinery.

The secondary function of the forward spin of the bomb now came into full effect.

The sides of the drum gripped the rippled surface of the concrete, and it accelerated across the flat space like a large, wide wheel, directly towards the wire mesh security fence at the far end, and crashed through it.

The bomb was deflected upwards at this point in its path, and it soared over the car park to the main control building.

Some of the sharp edges of the concrete had cut into the metal surface of the drum, tearing large gashes in the metal, and this had a terrifying effect on those who heard it.

The troops boarding the troopships on their way to the front line, the shipping workers and ship owners aligning the harbour dockside, and primarily of all, the various agencies utilizing the resources of the petroleum products which had supported the conflict for years gone by,

They all heard it.

Those who were outside in the streets had seen a black spinning object shrieking like a banshee, the pitch of the shrieks rising and falling as it wobbled and spun through the air.

It shrieked its way over the main refinery, the crude oil storage tanks, and started dropping down again towards the predetermined aiming point, which was now only a few hundred yards away.

Its penultimate bounce was through the plate glass windows and doors of the main operations control building.

Most of the forward momentum had gone now, but enough remained for it to bounce across the stainless steel mirrored reception area, and like one of the executives working within the building, it joined a group of people entering the lift for ascent to the top floor.

The lift operator, unfortunately for himself and the other occupants, had already pressed the button for the top floor and the express lift, with its unwelcome guest, rapidly shot up towards the top floor.

* * *

The internal timing device had been programmed to commence count down when the device had stopped moving, and was completely stationery.

However, the upwards movement delayed this operation until it reached the top of its ascent at the Executive Floor Level...

At which point the lift stopped its rapid climb, and the operator opened the doors to allow egress of occupants... which for some unaccountable reason they did in a very ungentlemanly and undignified fashion.

They had about ten seconds to make haste and exit the general area!

The small semiconductor started its count down. The ignition voltages for the trigger circuit had reached their required potential level...

And at the nine second mark a pulse pushed its way through the transmitter, linked to the satellite hovering above the Indian Ocean - which then transmitted a series of synchronized commands to the other four atomic devices, resting on the bed of the Strait of Hormuz.

It was at this precise moment that five thermonuclear hydrogen bombs,

Each with a capacity of one hundred and sixty megatons,

Exploded.

Chapter 14. Comeuppance

The combined shock waves of the five simultaneous explosions reverberated around the world for days, gradually diminishing in strength every hour, but they were picked up in micro-seconds by the ground, air and space-borne monitoring instruments.

The various operators around the world, who spend their entire lives looking at the output of these instruments, must have had a field day when they saw the results come out.

Most of them will be talking about that day for years to come, and boring the pants off their grandchildren well after that.

Cheltenham knew the results within five minutes, and the Prime Minister within six.

Within seven minutes the summons had been issued, and within eight minutes the Defence Secretary had received the expected phone call.

Two minutes after that the official car screeched to a halt outside his private house.

There were no courtesies.

The private secretary, and the two very large plain clothes gentlemen who were there 'for the Defence Secretary's protection', stormed through his front door straight into his study.

"Good afternoon gentlemen, can I assist you?" He asked elegantly.

The private secretary responded.

"Good afternoon Sir, I wonder if you could come with us now.

The Prime Minister is most anxious to see you."

"Of course, just a moment please,"

He turned to his writing bureau, opened the front flap and took out his letter.

He had typed it himself, as soon as he had received the phone call.

He read it once more to ensure that the correct protocol had been adhered to, folded it neatly; then took out one of his ministerial envelopes, placed it in carefully, and sealed it.

He opened his empty briefcase, placed the letter inside then closed the lid.

His personal secretary picked it up and went out to the car.

There was a clothes brush lying on the side table. He used it to brush a piece of fluff from the lapel of his morning coat.

His bowtie was slightly crooked.

He adjusted it to perfect fit.

There was a small piece of dirt on toecap of the patent leather shoe on his right foot. He bent down to inspect it. It was a small lump of mud from the front door mat.

How infuriating!

The top right hand drawer of his bureau fortunately held a clean duster so he took it out in order to wipe it off.

"Sir, I beg you, the Prime Minister is waiting," urged the private secretary.

The Defence Secretary looked at him.

"I do appreciate your concern, but please try and understand...

If this is to be my last day in the Ministry of Defence, then I intend to maintain my high standards right to the end."

He placed his shoe on a shoe rest at the side of the table, wiped the mud off the toe cap, gave it a final polish, folded the duster carefully then replaced it back in the drawer.

He then checked his dress in the long mirror beside the wall, picked up his white gloves and top hat, and turned to face his 'visitors'.

"Shall we go, gentlemen?"

The private secretary led the way, the Defence Secretary followed with the two policemen behind.

They used one car, and were at the front of Number Ten within two minutes.

The duty uniformed policeman saluted him as they entered.

"Would you please follow me, Sir?"

The private secretary led the way to the Cabinet Room door and waited outside.

The Defence Secretary made a final adjustment to his tie in the wall mirror, nodded to the secretary and was ushered in.

* * *

The Prime Minister was sitting at the centre of the table stretching down the room.

He walked across the carpet to a position directly opposite her, placed his briefcase on the table, took out his letter and placed it on the silver salver which had been positioned previously for his benefit.

He then closed his case and stood, with dignity, his gloves in his left hand, gazing at the wall immediately above her head.

She looked down at the tray.

"I'll deal with that later", she remarked coldly.

"Tell me first, Defence Secretary, in words of one syllable, exactly what went wrong?"

He maintained his composure.

"Prime Minister, nothing went wrong.

Everything operated to plan."

She glared at him.

"Then tell me, Defence Secretary, who gave the authorisation for the release of five nuclear devices?"

He cleared his throat.

"You did, Prime Minister."

If looks could kill, the Defence Secretary would have been dead by now.

She nearly spat the words out.

"I most certainly did not!"

Her hands were resting in front of her on the table.

"Prime Minister, I have in my personal notes dated 16th July, a private meeting in this room between ourselves, when you agreed to the use of five old atomic devices for mine clearance purposes."

She slowly stood up, straightened her arms and leant forward on her outstretched fingers, her eyes blazing in fury.

Her face was six inches from his.

She forced the words through her teeth which were clenched in anger.

"I agreed to the use of five old atomic weapons in the Strait of Hormuz for mine clearance purposes only.

I most certainly did not authorise the use of any thermonuclear device against the Bandar Abbas refinery and oil fields."

The last words were indeed spat out.

The Defence Secretary removed the silk handkerchief from the top pocket of his jacket, wiped his face then regained his composure.

* * *

The door to the Cabinet Room suddenly opened and the Leader of The Opposition walked in.

He quietly closed it behind him, walked slowly across the carpet and stood beside the Defence Secretary.

He glared coldly across the table:

"Prime Minister,

Am I to understand from your most recent conversation with the Defence Secretary,

That you authorised the clandestine use of five atomic weapons,

And that they detonated in the Strait of Hormuz this afternoon?"

She looked at him.

Then across to the Defence Secretary, then back to him again.

Her mouth opened, but she couldn't say a thing.

She was speechless.

She knew then that she was beaten.

Her shoulders dropped and she slumped back into her chair.

* * *

She pressed a button on the table top just beside her right hand.

The door to the Cabinet Room opened.

She looked at both of them.

Not a movement. Not a flicker. They were like two statues as they watched her.

"Yes, Prime Minister?" queried her private secretary.

She looked up at them as she spoke.

"Would you please contact the Palace and send Her Majesty my compliments.

Please advise her Personal Private Secretary that I will be sending her my letter of resignation on the grounds of ill health within the hour.

Please see to the necessary administration, and bring the letter to me for my attention as soon as possible.

Thank you."

Her secretary appeared stunned.

"Yes, Prime Minister," and made to go out of the door.

She turned round again and paused.

"Madam, I'm very sorry." Then closed the door after her.

The Prime Minister looked at both of them long and hard, then those cold eyes glared at the Defence Secretary.

Her eyes met his and momentarily flicked downwards towards the table.

He glanced down at the thirty ounce solid sterling silver salver, upon which rested his own letter, now enclosed in a crisp clean white envelope bearing the House of Commons crest.

He cleared his throat, bent forward and picked it up.

He looked straight into her eyes, as he very carefully placed it in front of her, the makings of a smile on his face.

"Madam", he said elegantly, "I have prepared the letter for you.

All it requires now is your signature."

And with that, the Defence Secretary, followed by the Leader of the Opposition, walked out of the room.

EPILOGUE

So, the whole operation was a set-up.

An unofficial venture to clear the Strait of Hormuz, and strike a blow right into the financial heart of Reddex, by hitting their oil fields and refinery.

The PM was used for the initial start up; and we, the two grey-haired expendables, five old atomic devices 'tweaked up' a bit, an old aeroplane, and a lot of good luck managed to pull it off.

The Strait is now cleared from all underwater devices, and the Gulf is now in use; but the northern end is still 'Aqua non Grata' due to a bit of residual radiation, which was one of the objectives in the first place.

The oil fields and the refinery are off limits for a few more years, depending on the half-life of the material that went 'bang'.

The experts disagree on the time factor, but Ray and I won't be around when it's finally cleared up.

It is now two years since we dropped the Hormuz bombs. I've often been asked how Ray and I feel about what we did.

It's very difficult to explain, and impossible to write down.

Some people tell us that we were doing our job as good soldiers should, and others just spit in our faces as soon as they see us.

Unfortunately, there's no happy medium with human nature.

You can only do what you think is best at the time and no more.

Everybody was an expert after the raid, when they could look back with hindsight at all the available facts, especially the 'armchair experts'; and we met a lot of them in our travels.

I have often tried to put feelings on paper but it's impossible.

It can't be done and even if I could, none of you reading this would be able to empathise, because you were not there at the time, and were not personally involved.

Even the thousands of RAF and USAF aircrew who lived with the bomb in the sixties and seventies must have wondered what it would have been like to drop the weapons that they trained with… and if they had used them, then the policies that they stood for would have failed.

The only people who can truly understand are those members of the American B29 crews who dropped the atomic bombs on Hiroshima and Nagasaki during the Second World War.

I think they must feel as we do. Very mixed feelings indeed.

Was it right to do what we did? Nobody can tell us.

We both have to tell ourselves that it was in a justifiable cause but who defines a justifiable cause?

So how did we achieve what is known as 'closure'?

Both Ray and I paid a visit to each of the Japanese cities as soon as we could, and paid our respects at the Hiroshima Bell.

It was a very moving experience, and we both felt that something else was needed for us, our generation, and future generations in remembrance.

So what did 'They who must be obeyed' carry out at our request, in respect for the hundreds of thousands who died directly because of what we did?

Well, next time you are in England, or, if you live in the British Isles, go to the City of Lincoln, and take a taxi or the bus to Fulbeck village.

Ray and I always go there when we visit the UK.

We've never missed a visit yet or likely to do so.

It's a poignant reminder of past events.

The village is exactly the same as it was on that fateful day when we flew over it.

It's black and charred and burnt as a lasting memento; but with a difference.

It has now been taken over by the British Services War Graves Commission, and is surrounded by a wide lawn of soft smooth grass, maintained by the local residents.

Around the whole memorial village is a white gravel pathway, and a six feet high wall built in Lincolnshire stone.

Set into the wall, at regular intervals all around the inside are white marble crosses, one for every resident of the village who perished.

At the northern gateway is the Book of Remembrance, set in a glass-fronted case, and the pages are turned daily for all to see.

In front of the gate is a ten feet high angel, with its wings fully outstretched,

Carved in black marble, its arms reaching forward, holding two white doves in its cupped hands,

Gazing forlornly at the distant twin towers of Lincoln Cathedral on the horizon.

* * *

The angel is standing on a square plinth of plain white marble, with inscriptions on each side in three inch high lettering, inlaid with gold; which you can read you walk around it, alternately in English, then in Arabic:-

FULBECK

Twinned With

BANDAR ABBAS

(Friendship Towns)

Acknowledgements

I would like to acknowledge the help and assistance given to me during the production of the manuscript by the following people.

Mrs Maureen Burton for her constant encouragement, medical information, patience and editing.

Andrew Burton for keyboarding and editing.

Bruce Ward (Tresham) for computer assistance.

Dennis Carlton for weapons and combat information.

George Chambers (Tresham) for weapons and combat information.

Doctor Pirzada for computer operating assistance.

James Burton for electronic advice

Neil Haxton for proof reading.

John Burton for proof reading.

Michael Williams for proof reading.

AUTHOR'S NOTE

I was inspired to write this story during August 1987 when the British Government made the decision to send four hunter type minesweepers from the United Kingdom to the Persian Gulf in support of the Royal Navy's Armilla operations to protect British registered shipping. The story is entirely fiction and it should be appreciated that some of the ideas within are pure figments of the imagination and should be treated as such.

Like all good stories, it is based on factual information and very topical events. True life has a habit of catching up on fiction and it is sad to see that some of the events depicted in the story have already happened since I first put pen to paper in the summer.

Without spoiling the story, I refer to the call up age for children in Iran which is now at ten years of age for initial military training, the continual supply of weapons and equipment to the area due to the disagreement of a total arms embargo and the escalation of shipping losses, particularly tankers, including British registered vessels.

I sincerely hope that the true life stops at this point.

When you have finished the book you may all send your extremely large cheques of appreciation so that I may retire to the Bahamas with my co author.

Until the next story, I bid you good reading.

The places within this story are real and many readers will recognise them and most of the people within are fictitious. Nothing is true, it is completely made up and set in the future so as not to offend anyone who considers events personal and reference to anything that has been done or doing.

It is meant to be a good entertaining read.

Tony Burton. RAF retired & revulcanised.

Two Chimneys. Christmas 1987.

Ex AEO Vulcan Mk1.

Ex Co-Pilot Vulcan Mk2.

Ex Captain Vulcan Mk2.

Editor's Note

My dad originally wrote his story 'The Straits of Hormuz' in 1987, and he presented a folder with it proudly printed out to me and each of my brothers.

After he died in 2006, my mum asked me to look through the files on his computer, to see if there was anything important that I needed to save, and I found some of the chapters from his book, that he had redrafted to account for the technological and geopolitical changes that had occurred in the two decades since he first wrote out his story. He had also changed the name of the story to 'Dire Straits'.

I created this first book, 'Dire Straits - The Choke Point' by editing the chapters he had been working on before he died, and finishing the story by transcribing and editing the missing chapters, using the folder he presented me with in 1987.

The second book in the series, 'Dire Straits - the Ultimate Choice' completes his story, and is completely transcribed and edited from the 1987 folder - I made no attempt to redraft or update these chapters, to avoid losing dad's 'voice', but this does mean that the timeline is completely wibbly-wobbly, and there are definitely some anachronisms - but who cares - the story still works, and this is after all fiction, not history.

Dad never spoke about his thoughts and emotions of being a part of Britain's nuclear attack V Force, but on reading some of the philosophising of his fictional alter-ego Peter Barten, I think that we are getting an insight into his deeper feelings about that part of his life.

I hope you enjoy dad's story.

John Burton, March 2024.

Dedicated to Tony Burton

much loved and missed

(15/04/1940 - 22/03/2006)

Printed in Great Britain
by Amazon